ONE SEASON

A NOVEL

ALAN WHITE

Inquiries should be addressed to:
Longbeard, LLC
P.O. Box 396
Stapleton, AL 36578
www.oneseasonbook.com

The Intellect logo is a trademark of Intellect Publishing, LLC.
www.IntellectPublishing.com

ISBN-978-1-945190-16-2

Cover Art design by Christine LaGrassa
Cover Photograph by Alan Cathey
Author Photograph by Barbara White
Manufactured in the United States of America

DEDICATION

To my father, John Joe White, who did not hunt turkeys but encouraged a boy to believe ... in himself.

ACKNOWLEDGMENTS

A special thanks to Barbara for her patience, help and love. To Tom Kelly for taking time with me for no good reason and for allowing me to include him and his quotes in a chapter. Lastly, to the wild turkey, who has taught me that man is not necessarily God's most complicated creature.

FOREWORD

There was a period, back during the early stages of the recovery of the wild turkey, when turkeys were limited to three states. Those were Alabama, Mississippi and Arkansas and two of these seasons, except for Alabama, were very short.

One Season takes the reader through a single season, early in the period during the time of reestablishment, when populations were low. Very few people had any interest in talking about turkey tactics and techniques and those who did were mostly unwilling to share any information, especially to a raw recruit, because they preferred to save it for themselves.

Any information that came from outside was highly suspect. Anything that came from inside, even from members of your own family was, in many cases, tarred with the same brush.

Nobody, and by that I mean nobody, gave away a thing. The "boy" in this story is blessed with an honest and benevolent grandfather who learned the hard way.

Alan covers very well what has come to be called "The bad old days" when you mostly made it on your own or you didn't make it at all.

This is how it really was. If you came along after this period, be happy you missed it. You didn't miss a damn thing.

Tom Kelly

ONE SEASON

A NOVEL

"As you do not know the way of the spirit, nor how the bones grow in the womb of a woman with child, even so you do not know the work of God who maketh it all."

-Ecclesiastes 11:5.

CHAPTER 1 – OPENING DAY

The old man's bare feet touched the cool wooden floor. The crickets outside the window made their last attempt at calling a mate before dawn. Their singing, the only sound he heard. The alarm clock had not yet erupted with its incessant clatter. The man pushed the button on the back of the clock to make sure he wouldn't have to hear it. After so many years of waking up without it, there was little need any more to set the thing, but he did it anyway in case the internal clock in his mind failed him.

Today especially, Joe Parker did not want to be late.

He padded quietly into the kitchen to fumble with the coffee maker. Once he added water to brew a three-cup pot, he went to the bathroom to splash cold water on his whiskered face. He combed his hair while thinking … *just to make sure I don't scare any small children.* He smiled. *That line always made Maggie laugh.*

Joe didn't expect to encounter any children today. He slipped on faded green pants, a brown shirt and a faded, well-worn camouflage vest. Pulling a cap on his head, he returned to the kitchen to pour coffee into a cup. The remainder of the black liquid went into the stainless thermos on the counter. He knew it would get cold by nine AM.

But, cold coffee is better than nothing.

In case he got the job done by seven, he would celebrate with a hot cup back in the truck.

Belle had patience. The old spaniel sat quietly on the kitchen floor, gazing up at the man, steadily wagging her tail. She knew she could rely on him. The old man leaned over and poured a cup of dry food into her bowl, which she began to eat.

His mind drifted to his grandson. The boy had become troubled since his father's death.

Connor needs a steady, guiding hand. He's only fourteen.

He longed for Saturday when, for the first time in six months, the boy would visit.

Spring Break, or some such excuse for schools to close for a week, started in two more days. This year, the boy would spend it with the old man who thought about the boy often.

He tucked the thermos under his arm and balanced the shotgun over his shoulder as he strolled out to the truck, cup in hand. A quick glance at the night sky revealed a light, low fog, but a few stars showed through. The air smelled like creek water.

Good things come to those who wait.

Months ago, the waiting had started. Alabama's turkey season ended each year on April twenty-fifth. After the season, Joe was afforded a few months to relax. In October, he'd begun subconsciously waiting. The spring turkey season, the cause of his anticipation, seemed far away.

He'd filled the time with other pursuits. Growing vegetables, fishing, maintaining the small farm, and deer, quail, and dove hunting. All the while, he was gathering information about the past spring's hatch and checking flock numbers, which were looking good. By January, the waiting had developed into restlessness.

To Joe and a few special men, who some may call obsessed, wild turkeys are not simply game animals. They are not mere birds. They are much more. Majestic, mysterious creatures that cannot be classified among others.

4

The interaction between certain humans who have managed to match wits with them in the wild cannot be dismissed as simply hunting. It is more a spiritual encounter than a rendezvous with any other animal. Only through many years' experience, encounters, and sensitivity to such things could a person truly know this. Even then, it could not be adequately explained with words.

However, it was to no purpose for Joe to ponder such things today. The morning of March twentieth, nineteen sixty-nine, had arrived—opening day of the season—with a calm wind. Little else mattered to Joe that morning.

The drive to the Hall Place, twenty-two minutes on county roads filled with potholes, lay ahead. Joe loved the four-hundred-fifty acres of mixed hardwoods and pines and the small creek it contained. A power line ran through it, sixty yards wide. Joe had acquired access to many parcels of land with turkey hunting privileges over the years. The reason he chose to start the season there was simply tradition.

For the last two decades he had opened the season at the same location. This year he knew, from previous scouting trips, at least three mature gobblers were there. He had seen them two weeks prior on the power line with a group of hens. Only one of the gobblers had been strutting which meant he was probably the dominant bird.

Through the binoculars, the "boss" appeared to be a worthy opponent. He would save the younger gobblers for the boy.

Yep, younger gobblers are better for training. They gobble more and will come to a call much easier than an old, seasoned warrior will.

Joe had plans for turkey hunting with the boy during his visit this time.

CHAPTER 2 – GAME ON

The metal gate, wet with fog from the night, cooled his fingers as he unlocked it before easing it to the side to drive his truck through the gap. After driving the truck through, he closed the gate and locked it, then drove another hundred yards to the place he always parked. When the engine fell silent, he waited with the windows down to drink in the cool, wet, morning air while finishing the last sip from his cup.

He reached over to feel the slick wooden forearm of the double-barrel twenty-gauge. Joe hunted with this gun the last twenty-three seasons, over half of his turkey hunting years. It showed the wear from years of service. He considered giving it up to buy a new gun a few years ago, when the front sight was accidentally broken off, but he couldn't do it. He had the sight replaced at a sporting goods store in Monroeville by a part-time gunsmith. Joe decided it was once again sufficient for the purpose to which assigned. The weapon had become as familiar in his hands as his own wrinkled skin. He saw no practical reason to change it. Nor did he see any way it could be improved.

His thoughts turned to a time-honored truism: *Waste not, want not.*

The Depression had taught him some hard lessons. He'd left high school after the tenth grade, to help put food on his family's table. No regrets. It was just the way things were.

He stepped outside, pulling the gun alongside and easing shut the truck's faded blue door. The modern world melted away behind him. The ancient world lay ahead. A smile settled in his eyes. He inhaled a long breath and his skin prickled a little, after all the years ... anticipation. He slipped two number-four shells into the barrels without glancing down, his eyes still on the pale eastern sky.

Stepping carefully down the pig-trail road in the dark, he heard the first owl in the creek bottom at a half mile away. When he arrived at the place to exit the trail, he stopped, waiting for more light before attempting to weave through the dogwoods, oaks and pines along the hillside. The ridge stretched for three-quarters of a mile above the edge of the swamp. Dew had smothered the leaves and sticks on the ground, allowing him to tread silent and steady.

Good things come to those who wait.

The fog lifted somewhat as the sky shifted for the arriving of dawn. Tendrils of the remaining fog enveloped the woodland and the swamp. Five minutes passed with no sound from the owls as he began his slow, systematic sneak to "the place."

The place would mean nothing to other men. It possessed no landmarks, remaining private and only known to him ... intimately. A certain tree there, a huge longleaf pine, provided the sitting place. For the last several years, this had been where he opened the season. It was special only to him and would have been of no consequence to another human on earth. All the necessities for him, put there by Mother Nature years ago, afforded him a comfortable place to sit with the right amount of slant to the ground. A natural blind of small plants surrounded the place, high enough to conceal him but not too high to prevent a clean shot at the gobbler he hoped to call. The plants never seemed to grow any taller from year to year, as if some unknown woodland gods kept the place in excellent order … just for Joe.

A spectacular view with a canopy of high shade overhead—forty yards of sparse openings on three sides: front, left and right—provided a perfect view of any approaching creatures. The place, seventy-five yards from where the land began to drop into the creek bottom, created an area perfect for a turkey to fly, land, and strut before coming the rest of the way to the gun, which had a clean killing range of thirty yards.

Joe's Celtic ancestors would have referred to the area as a "thin place;" certain locations where the boundaries between heaven and earth are especially thin … a place where one can sense the Divine more readily.

With some effort and pain from his knees, he sat down on the ground with his back to the tree trunk. He wiggled-in his backside to the soft ground, carefully removing the box call from his vest. He placed the diaphragm call on his lap, pulled a green bandana up onto his nose, lowered the cap to his eyebrows and balanced the gun on his left knee with the stock slightly under his right arm. The owl called again in the distance. He smiled because he knew he would not have to sound an owl call this morning to cause a turkey to gobble. The real thing was on duty, doing that job just fine. The light brightened in the eastern sky. A cardinal trilled. The game had begun.

While he waited, he allowed his thoughts to wander to the boy. The loss of his father six months ago had been a cruel turn of events. He couldn't pretend to know what the boy was going through. He knew it had been bad.

Joe's only daughter reported that Connor had been troubled. The boy's anger had manifested itself with frequent fights at school.

But what use is an old man in such matters as these?

The yearning to help pulled heavily on his heart. Two more days to wait, then he would know more.

CHAPTER 3 – MANEUVERS

He gently picked up the box call and made two short, very soft clucks in case a turkey was close. He slowly eased the call back to the ground by his side, before carefully cradling the stock of the gun with his right hand. The woods fell silent. He waited.

To his right at two hundred yards, from the depths of the creek bottom, the thunder of the first gobbler seemed to shake the leaves. The raspy, high-pitched gobble echoed along the ridge. The old man remained motionless.

Meanwhile, other types of birds greeted the sunrise. Chirping and flitting about and alerting their neighbors, they announced their presence as if they'd been away for years. Scurrying from one limb to the other, they seemed to be completely unorganized in an effort to make sure they could still fly. The sounds of the new spring day filled the morning.

The gobbler rang out a second time without provocation and another answered from somewhere far across the creek. Glad he was here one more time, one more season, one more opening day, Joe's eyes twinkled. Three minutes slowly passed as the smaller creatures continued their noises until the woods filled with one long, continuous mixture of bird sounds. The deep woods had come to life.

To the left, down in the bottom, a deep roaring gobble rose from the swamp. This one, different than the others. The turkey that the old man would match wits with had finally spoken.

The one that had left his track in the sandy ruts of the nearby roadbeds and placed his strutting marks at the upper part of the field.

There he is.

When the boss sounded again, the woods reverberated, reminding the old man of a lion's roar he'd once heard in the Memphis zoo. The deep hollow where the turkey roosted served as a sound reflector, like the box of a guitar. The old gobbler must have known this, claiming the roosting spot for that reason. The other creatures of the woods seemed to hush in response to the sound of the boss tom making it known who was in charge. The old man breathed deep.

He reached down to the box call on the ground without picking it up, gently pulling the lid across the box, making a purr that he could barely hear. He followed that with an equally soft three-yelp sequence, all in a perfect cadence. The gobbler answered in a strong manner, demanding any other gobbler thinking about gobbling to shut up and stay that way.

The boss is "on the job site and working."

The old man slowly moved his right hand back to the gun, gripped it gently and adjusted the forearm slightly on his left knee. He eased the stock against the front of his shoulder.

The work's done. The rest is up to the ole bird.

He waited in perfect contentment. After ten minutes, a limb cracked in the direction of the gobbler. Joe imagined the boss sailing from his roost, gliding silently through the air, softly touching down on the forest floor. Joe recognized a limb cracking indicated a gobbler had pitched off a limb. He could only hope the tom had flown to his side of the creek.

Joe fought the strong urge to call again. To make the turkey gobble again, revealing his location, would be satisfying. But old, wise turkeys were not killed that way. The gobbler would come if it was meant to be, and Joe knew that's all there was to it now.

The sound of a hen, the soft morning tree yelps or the fly-down cackle, had not been heard.

I'm sure they're here but they ain't called yet.

Joe's first glimpse of the boss revealed only his head. Blue as a robin's egg, it drifted between two young post oaks at one hundred yards away before melting into the understory. The boss maneuvered parallel to the creek. Its present course would bring the turkey between Joe and the swamp edge to his immediate front. Joe smiled again. To coax this creature within sight, without being discovered, sent a thrilling shiver along his spine. No matter how many times it happened, it always filled him with as much tingling excitement as it had the first time he ever did it.

The next time Joe saw the boss, the bird materialized from the foggy shadows at seventy-five yards, still sauntering parallel to the creek, his motion so smooth he seemed to float across the landscape. Joe considered the tom's persona every bit as graceful as Audrey Hepburn, Maggie's favorite movie star.

At this distance, the old man could "feel" its presence as he watched the sway of the heavy beard with each step the turkey made. A chill traveled though the man's bones. The boss issued a challenge with each deliberate, heavy step. The gobbler paused, hoisting his shiny black shroud of feathers around him. His tail fan spread wide as he strutted.

Then, Joe heard the drumming.

The low-frequency, guttural hum made the hairs on the back of Joe's neck stand up. Joe saw the turkey's head tucked neatly in the center of his big chest and felt the vibrato of its drumming under his ribs and inside his chest cavity. Vibrations were felt as well as heard.

The gobbler stopped in a spot that held the first bit of morning light to reach the ground after filtering through the tree canopy. The boss's feathers reflected the sunlight and emitted multiple colors to emanate from what, just a few seconds ago, stood solid black. Bright sparkles of green, bronze, orange, and iridescent colors of all hues radiated from the bird.

The turkey gobbled in unexpected vehemence. It startled Joe, almost causing the gun to hop off the old man's skinny kneecap. From the corner of his right eye, Joe caught movement between himself and the morning sky. A hen sailed from a tree somewhere behind Joe's right shoulder, almost landing on top of the gobbler. The gobbler turned its strutting body to face the hen as another hen silently sailed the same path to blend with the two.

The first hen came ten yards toward Joe, scrutinizing him, then cackled. It sounded as close to a turkey cussing another turkey that he could imagine. Her attention locked Joe in place with no way to move without one of three sets of eyes catching him. Worse yet, the gobbler remained just beyond gun range. The hens, having heard Joe's ambiguous earlier call, must have considered this strange, unseen turkey to be an unwelcome guest at the courtship ritual. The old hen let her feelings be known to this invisible intruder before promptly sashaying close to the gobbler.

The old man relaxed. He recognized any chance of the gobbler coming closer now were slim. The hens began to peck at the ground and scrabbled in the direction from where the gobbler had approached. The boss followed. Within a minute, the group of turkeys vanished.

When Joe yelped a call again, the hens answered him quickly a hundred yards away. The next time they answered his call, they had traveled farther. By this, he determined they had retreated along the edge of the drop-off into the creek bottom and were heading toward the power line.

The old man rose from his position, grimacing with pain from his knees. Getting up from the ground had once been as easy as blinking his eyes but age had slowed most movements that once he had taken for granted. Years of climbing power poles at his job had been hard on his knees. Many of his lineman friends already had knee-replacement surgery.

He knew where the turkeys were headed but could he beat them there? He would try. He thought if he were younger he could easily jog to the edge of the power line ahead of them, wait for them to arrive and maybe have a chance to kill the tom when the group emerged into the opening where wild clover and the safety of an open space awaited. But, at his age, he could only hope to step fast enough to beat them there.

He eased away from the creek, following an old fireguard around to the power line clearing while keeping plenty of distance between where he believed the turkeys to be. He arrived at the power line's edge, stopping to ease closer. He figured the group would most likely emerge close to where the land began to descend into the creek bottom.

Seeing no signs of the turkeys, he sneaked along the edge of the clearing to make his way toward his destination. When he came within sixty yards of the crest leading to the bottomland, he stopped a few yards from the edge of the clearing to sit under a small holly tree. The tree's lower limbs extended just high enough to allow him to sit underneath them, making a natural dark, shady spot that provided a little more camouflage from the rising sun's light against his clothing. The setup worked well enough on such short notice.

After pulling the diaphragm call from his vest pocket, he placed it on top of his tongue and squeezed out a series of cuts and yelps. The sound mimicked an excited hen who wanted to join the group. The hens answered just inside the wood line directly in front of him. Five turkeys emerged onto the power line's edge. Four hens arrived first, with the big tom following behind. The hens became interested in investigating the new turkey as Joe called again with a soft purr. He quickly followed with a cluck. Four hens turned, as one began to head directly toward Joe. With his right thumb, he eased the hammer to full cock before snugging his cheek against the stock.

The tom watched the hens as they went to investigate the invisible turkey. He dropped out of his strut and gobbled directly into the backside of four hens as if expressing his opposition to the route they had chosen. The hens kept stepping towards Joe. The gobbler regained his strut, resigning himself to follow the curious hens. Slower to shift direction, he fell behind the hens by about twenty yards. The first hen, within ten yards of Joe, became uneasy, shifting into a side-stepping, head-bobbing, clucking dance in front of the gun barrel while moving in between Joe and the gobbler. The old man aligned the front sight with the gobbler's head, before tonguing the diaphragm call to create a sharp cluck. The rebuffed hens scurried toward the middle of the power line, clearing away from the unwelcome sound, as the gobbler raised his head, becoming curious.

The full load of number fours rammed the turkey in the neck. The heavy turkey rolled backward to settle motionless on a patch of clover.

The old man breathed normally for the first time since daylight.

Joe relaxed the back of his head against the little trunk of the holly tree as his cheeks rose to crinkle his eyes in a long, pleasant smile. His eyes moistened. He stretched his legs before rising to approach the bird.

15

Joe knelt to place his hand on the turkey's back. He admired the bird's long spurs, sharp as needles. He gathered the beard in the palm of his hand and smoothed it out. His eyes tightened as a twinge of sadness ran through him that the hunt had ended.

Forty-five years had passed since his first hunt for wild turkey. The love for the pursuit had never faltered. With a spring of energy like reinvigorated youth, he hoisted the heavy turkey by the legs, swinging it over his shoulder to start the long slog toward the truck.

The coffee might still be hot.

The old man took his time strolling through the woods to the truck as a tug of melancholy pulled at him at leaving these woods today. A few days would pass and the next boss tom would find his voice and claim the area.

He would let the area rest. Until then, his spirit soared with the joy of a new season coupled with an exceptional "opening day" kill. It had been several years since he'd bagged a tom on opening day. The turkey population was improving. Joe had other places to hunt in the coming days.

CHAPTER 4 – THE CALL

The Broken Arrow café did not have a reputation for culinary delights. However, it was only two miles from Joe's home as well as the only café within fifteen miles where a decent breakfast was served.

The café in Uriah, pronounced "U-ri" by locals, sat beside Highway 21 across from the feed store. The community sported one grocery called The Big Store, one gas station and two small diners, but only one that opened for breakfast.

The café's cook fixed his eggs, grits and bacon the way Joe liked them. The old man anticipated treating himself to a full plate before cleaning the bird.

When he stopped the truck in front of the café, he noticed only one other truck parked there. Glen Pace, a local farmer, sat at the front table. The long table for twelve diners served as the community table where most local folks sat with one another to carry on conversations over hot coffee and fat biscuits.

"Mornin', Glen, how ya doing?" Joe said as he pulled out a chair.

"Dang, Joe, you ain't huntin' today? Ain't this opening day for turkey?" Glen asked with a laugh.

"Yep, already been."

"Oh … well, you musta' got one early."

"Yep, got lucky today."

17

"Lucky, my foot! I know better'n that. You could kill a turkey in Bienville Square in downtown Mobile if he gobbled on Royal Street."

Joe laughed. He liked Glen, even though the man didn't hunt turkeys and didn't want to start. Glen didn't understand why anyone would. But, he always wanted to hear about it, seeming genuinely interested in what he considered a few very curious fellers who did it.

"Good one?" Glen said.

"A fine one."

"Well, good for you."

Joe raised the coffee cup to his mouth. "Thanks, Glen."

Earlier, the waitress had poured a cup of coffee as soon as she saw Joe's truck drive into the parking lot. A plate glass window served as the front of the café. She did not need to ask if he wanted coffee. She knew what he liked to drink as well as how he liked his eggs fried, and she had the coffee waiting on the table by the time he took his seat.

While Joe ate, he spoke with Glen about the rain and the cost of fertilizer, then listened with boredom as Glen explained how all the hippies were causing the United States to go to hell in a hand basket.

Joe paid his bill at the register, dropped the change in the tip jar, all the while knowing as he climbed into the truck Glen would make sure the whole town knew about the gobbler he'd killed that morning. Not that it mattered to him. He found it amusing.

Back home, after Joe finished cleaning the turkey, he placed most of the breast and thighs in the deep freezer. The fan, with its beautiful feathers, would be dried by using borax, then added to the display of fans lining the inside of his barn. The beard and spurs would also be saved to honor the bird, while serving as a reminder of the hunt. He would show them to Connor on Saturday.

Afterward, he went inside, washed his hands, and sat down in his favorite chair to enjoy a short rest. The soft sofa chair enveloped his body like a familiar blanket. Beside it, a framed photo of his late wife sat on a table. Sitting for a while before the day's chores got started, he was comforted by the familiar surroundings.

The tomato, bell pepper and squash plants he'd set out a few days ago required tending. He knew they would need a layer of pine straw placed around them to keep the soil moist. The peach trees, not quite in bloom, could be safely sprayed with insecticide before they flowered. Laundry and other household chores needed attention.

He considered the day would still allow time for scouting at the Thompson Tract, a cattle farm that he'd hunted for several years up Highway 59, one thousand fifty-six acres, over half of which were pastures. Always a reliable place for turkeys, a week ago he'd found gobbler tracks in the edge of one pasture and others on an old road at the backside of the property. Depending on what he saw today, he might go there in the morning.

For thirty-five years of his life, Joe Parker had worked as a lineman for the rural electric co-op. Although it was hard work, he enjoyed the job. The years finally caught up with him, so he retired. It was a good job, offering him the opportunity to meet just about every homeowner in the county during those years. Some of them, who had discovered he liked to hunt turkeys, gave him permission to hunt their lands.

During the last fifteen years on the job, he had risen to a supervisor position. It allowed him to choose his working hours. Every spring he would work from ten AM to seven PM, which allowed time for turkey hunting in the mornings before work.

He and Maggie had one child, a girl, who they named Nancy after Maggie's favorite aunt. When Maggie died of cancer five years ago, he found himself alone except for Belle. A spaniel mix, getting old herself, Belle was a constant companion for the last twelve years. Belle followed Joe everywhere within the forty-acre farm he still maintained. However, Belle moved a little slower these days … as did Joe.

The day boasted beautiful spring weather. The old man set about his chores. After a midday nap, and tending to the chickens, garden and chores, he decided to skip the scouting trip. At five-thirty he went back in the house to begin preparing supper when the telephone rang.

The rotary dial black phone still hung on the wall of the hallway since being installed there in nineteen forty-three. The house, new then, was built by Joe over a period of three years. With the cost of hiring a contractor to build it being out of reach on a lineman's pay, Joe had little choice if he wanted a house of his own. On Labor Day, in nineteen thirty-seven, he laid the first cement blocks for the foundation. Joe built as the money became available.

Many sacrifices had been made back then to gain extra money for lumber, windows, shingles, plus all the other expenses that went along with building a house. He and Maggie were dedicated to the project. They worked to build the house together, with only a small loan from the bank to get the kitchen, master bedroom and bath finished so they could move in.

They finished the rest afterward with money saved on rent. Three years later, the house was completed.

He answered the phone on the second ring. "Hello?"

"Hey, Daddy, how ya doin?" Nancy said.

"Hey, sweet pea. I'm doing good, real good."

"Listen, I need to talk to you about Connor and his visit."

"I hope he's still coming. Is anything wrong?"

"No, no, he'll be there, but … well, you know he's had a hard time at school since James died. It just seems to get worse and worse. I'm at my wit's end. I wanted to see how you felt about an idea I have."

"Okay. I know the boy's been trying to adjust. Losing a father when you're only fourteen just ain't right. I know he's been in some trouble at school and all. I wish I could do something."

"Well, maybe you can. This school year ends in just a few months. Honestly, I think he'd be better off switching schools for the rest of this year. You know, a fresh start, new friends, different teachers. He's just so sad. And, this school situation is not helping. What do you think, Daddy?"

Joe could tell in his daughter's voice that tears would come soon. His heart ached when he thought of the pain she had endured.

"Honey, I would be happy to let him live with me for as long as you need. Don't you worry about a thing. I'll watch out for him real good."

"Daddy, I just think he needs a male guardian for a little while. I'm just not what he needs right now." Her voice quivering, "I feel so inadequate, but it's what *he* needs that's more important. You know?"

"I understand. Everything will be fine. Don't worry. You're a good mama. You're just going through a bad patch right now."

"Okay, Daddy. Well, he wants to talk to you, okay? I'll see you Saturday morning around ten."

"Okay, sweetheart. I love you."

Connor blurted into the phone, "Paw Paw, I want to live with you the rest of this year."

"Okay, son, we'll work on that with your mom."

"I hate this school. I want to go to school in Uriah."

"Well, come on up on Saturday with all your stuff. We'll get you settled in over Spring Break."

"Paw Paw, you still planning for us to turkey hunt?"

"Well, son, does a frog bump his butt when he hops? I can't wait to take you. And Connor, this year you're gonna try it on your own."

"Oh, cool. Really? You think I'll be ready?"

"No, but there's only one way to learn to turkey hunt on your own. Just go and try. That's the best way."

"But you're gonna help me some first, right?"

"Sure. I gotta get you ready, ain't I?"

"Yes, sir. I'll be there Saturday morning."

"You bet. See you then, buddy."

"Okay, Paw Paw. Bye."

Before the phone went dead, Joe heard his grandson yelling through the house to his Mom, "Mama, he's gonna let me—" Then the phone went dead.

The telephone had served to keep Joe in contact with his grandson over the years. Nancy called twice a week. Joe always asked to talk to Connor. Most of the calls were made after eight PM, when the long-distance charges were less. Joe planned for them.

Connor had been with Joe on several hunts for squirrel, deer and dove. A few turkey hunts over the last two years were taken, although spring visits were not common. Most visits had been long enough to afford the time for a morning or afternoon in the woods. In addition, he'd been with Joe on several fishing trips around the Alabama River system nearby.

The boy, enthusiastic about the outdoors, marveled at all the things Joe pointed out. Living in the city, these trips to the country had been a treat for Connor, but Joe noticed during the past two years the boy's curiosity took on a whole new level. He wanted to become a woodsman. This pleased Joe. However, he knew that becoming guardian of a teenage boy involved a lot more than teaching him wood lore.

After supper, Joe built a small fire in the front room fireplace to rid the house of the night's chill. He and the spaniel sat in silence together watching the flames, enjoying the warmth. He thought about his son-in-law, gone now for over six months, his daughter, and Connor.

How things change. How long has it been since I had a young one in the house?

He acknowledged how much he longed for the visit as he sat beside the fire.

Like turkey hunting, the prospect of what may come next is what keeps you going.

CHAPTER 5 – THREE'S A CROWD

The weather on the morning of March twenty-first was almost a mirror of the day before. After the morning's routine, Joe drove to the Thompson Tract.

The cattle farm bordered a creek along the western edge. It included a mixture of pastureland, tall stands of pine and bushy thickets. Historically, turkeys had chosen to roost near the creek but plenty of other suitable roosting hollows and drains littered the property. The cows, wandering around the place for years, had kept most of the underbrush to a minimum. The cow trails presented the turkeys and the hunter plenty of easy paths from one field to the other.

The stands of timber were occasionally control-burned. This year, forty acres that bordered the creek had been burned in January. The new green sprouts, along with lush grasses, blanketed the burned area and provided the wild turkeys a favorite place to feed as well as scrounge for bugs. Dried cow patties, another favorite food source, lay everywhere. A turkey would simply use one foot, flip the patty over, and peck the bugs and undigested corn stashed underneath.

Once Joe parked the truck, he began a long hike across a pasture. He headed west to the burn by the creek. He decided to begin the hunt at the upper edge of the burn with the pasture behind him. Plenty of pine trees as wide as his shoulders grew there, which helped to screen his shape from any tom turkey approaching him.

After selecting one, he pruned a few small bushes before daylight, and stuck them in the ground about six feet in front of where he would sit for a makeshift blind. He settled in. Just as the first redbird chirped, he hooted like a barred owl. The cadence of, "Who cooks for you, who cooks for you all?" He couldn't call as loud as he once could but in the quiet, windless morning air, the volume was more than sufficient.

Joe did not know why the sound of a barred owl caused some tom turkeys to respond with a gobble. He only knew it worked well. If you wanted to learn the location of your prey, just sound like a barred owl. He figured the owl and the wild turkey were natural enemies. Both possessed loud voices. He wondered if they were competing for dominance of the morning woodlands.

A gobbler answered as soon as the last note left Joe's chest. Then another. And then a third gobbler made his presence known. By the sound of the gobbles, he could tell the toms were evenly spread out along the creek in front of him, about two hundred yards away. One in the middle, one to the left and one to the right.

Perfect.

The toms continued to gobble at one another for the next ten minutes as Joe sat back, soaking in the sounds. Then Joe made the first hen call, a quick couple of loud *cuts* to mimic the sound of a hen excited by the tom's gobble. He followed this with a four-note mating yelp, an invitation to the gobbler for a rendezvous. The toms went crazy, gobbling with every breath.

"Y'all gonna wake up the whole county," Joe whispered aloud, chuckling.

With the shotgun in position, he strained to catch a sound, any shift in the air, as he rotated his head. He listened for the softest whisper of wing strokes that would lift the turkey from its roost to land at its chosen place on the ground. Twenty minutes passed before they stopped gobbling while readying to fly down.

Sometimes they just like to hear their own voices.

Joe figured he was now operating on "their time," not his.

Turkey time is different than human time.

In fact, he didn't think time even factored in the life of a turkey. They lived each moment to its fullest.

Nowhere to be and plenty of time to get there.

By the time the gobblers flew from their roost, he had heard at least three different hens calling to the south of his position. They were roosting over a small gully that ran east. After the toms gobbled from the ground, he made a second call almost identical to the first but followed by two distinct clucks. This, he hoped, would send a new message to the gobblers … I'm here, I'm interested in you but I'm happy where I am, so come on over for a visit … and, like most well-laid plans, it didn't work out exactly as he wanted.

These gobblers knew the voices of real hens. A sure thing is always the best choice. As they continued to gobble, they moved toward the location of the hens. The hens joined the trio of toms. Joe decided to try a last-ditch effort to try to coax the hens to him, hoping the gobblers would follow.

With the box call, he stroked a long series of yelps intended to aggravate the flock of hens to the point they would have to investigate this new, loud-mouthed hen trying to take away their gobblers.

The gobbling stopped as if someone flipped a switch. No sound from the hens either. Thirty minutes passed … then an hour … no sign of a living turkey. No sound of a turkey was heard, as if they'd been muted.

Joe surmised the hens had led the gobblers away from him. He shifted his position, stretching out his legs to let the blood flow to his feet for a while. He rolled to one side, raising himself up with his arms until he achieved a kneeling position, to survey behind his position and into the pasture. There they were. Three gobblers in full strut accompanied by five pecking hens had circled around him and entered the pasture behind. They stood in the middle of the pasture, one hundred fifty yards away.

He rose to stand a while, keeping the big pine trunk between himself and the flock of turkeys. He stretched his back, along with all the joints he could, without taking a step. He cautiously peeked around the tree very carefully to watch the gobblers do their best strutting for the hens.

One hen began running in small circles before squatting in the grass. Approaching her with careful steps, the lead gobbler pecked at the hen once or twice. He climbed on her back. The gobbler's wings flapped several times before he stepped away from her. He had bred the hen. After another minute, the hen rose and took a few quick steps away to resume pecking again as if nothing had happened.

Joe eased lower, crouching to his knees, crawling around the other side of the pine to sit again watching the field. He leaned his head against the tree and closed his eyes. *A nap is the only productive thing to do in this situation.*

His hunting experiences had taught him that until the hens left the gobblers behind, they would be right there, in the safety of the wide-open space where any predator daring to approach would be seen by eight sets of the best eyes on the planet. Joe dozed in fits and spurts for another hour. When he peeked under his eyelids the last time, he spotted the last hen evacuating the pasture. All three gobblers waited ... as forlorn as any jilted lover.

Joe rested the gun on his knee before he retrieved the box call. One cluck ... a second cluck ... then silence. That was all it took. All three gobblers relaxed out of strut, stretching their necks toward the sky to scan the wood line in Joe's direction. A gobbler took a step toward Joe. The other gobblers took two steps. Then the first gobbler … another step. All three broke into a run straight toward his gun barrel. They ran as fast as any turkeys he'd ever seen run, but when they got thirty yards from the edge of the pasture they all stopped dead-still. Joe heard their quiet clucks as the gobblers stepped back and forth to probe Joe's area with their eyes. The first one that went into strut boasted a ten-inch beard that spread three inches wide.

A paintbrush.

The other two also sported healthy beards. He estimated each turkey would weigh around seventeen pounds.

Joe eased his cheek to the smooth stock of the gun. He lined up the big turkey's neck, putting the front sight of the gun three inches below the head. He slid his thumb over the hammer to ease it to full cock position.

Then, Joe Parker whispered, "Boom."

Joe didn't pull the trigger, deciding to save these turkeys for Connor. Joe had accomplished everything except the kill.

He waited in position until all three gobblers moved out of sight to the north edge of the pasture. Gathering his calls, using the tree for support, he rose to his knees and then to his feet. He stretched his joints straight again before hiking back to the truck. His old thermos let the coffee get stone cold. Still, after a morning like this, he enjoyed every sip of it on the way to the cafe.

Chapter 6 – Change

Joe pulled into the parking area of the Broken Arrow at ten-thirty AM. Several men, mostly farmers, sat together having their midmorning coffee. During the conversation, one of the men, Earl Chatom, said, "A young feller was looking for you this mornin'. I think he had a turkey question. Didn't catch his name. Said he'd come back later."

"Okay," Joe replied.

"You hunt this morning?" Earl asked.

"Yep, it was a good morning, just couldn't tote him home today," Joe said. "He'll be there later. Hope to get the boy on him next week."

"Oh, you gettin' a visit?"

"Yeah, this time it might be a good, long visit."

When Joe paid for the coffee and stepped out the door, a green nineteen sixty-one Chevrolet pickup pulled into the parking lot. A young man lurched out calling, "Mr. Parker, you have a minute?"

Joe recognized the young man, with his shock of red hair, rawhide skin and tall, lean stature. "Hello, Daniel, how you been?"

"I'm fine, Mr. Parker, but I got a turkey giving me fits."

"Well, that ain't good. Tell me about it, son."

The young man spent the next fifteen minutes telling Joe about an old gobbler he'd encountered on opening day. Then again, this morning, with the same results. The turkey would come to various yelping calls, gobbling often. However, when the tom got within eighty yards, he'd stop, without coming any closer.

What the young man described resembled a common practice of a wise ole tom that had been hunted hard, possibly shot at and missed, becoming "call-shy." Hunters referred to a turkey that stopped before coming into gun range as "hanging up" or being "hung-up."

Joe offered Daniel two ideas to try on the bird to trick him into the gun's range. "In the morning, set up about fifty yards further away from his roost than you did today, make your regular call early, then move about seventy-five yards towards him quick without getting seen. Don't call again. Sit there to wait him out. Hopefully, he'll come closer thinking you are where you called from. He may get close enough for you to take a shot. The trick will be to slip toward him without him seeing you from his roost. That's why you need to call to him early before there's too much light. The more sunlight there is, the easier it is for the bird to see you.

"If that doesn't work, call him like usual, but when he hits the ground to start coming your way, walk straight away from him and call as you go further away. If you hear him following you, find a place where you can double back on him, sit down, be quiet and get him to walk by you."

The young man thanked Joe, promising to try those ideas. Joe liked giving advice to young hunters if they asked kindly and showed some respect for the bird. He knew Daniel's parents; they were good people. The young man would do the right thing when it came to hunting.

The sandy driveway off Rocky Hill Road leading to Joe's house was about a hundred yards long. Between the front yard and the wide, red-clay expanse of Rocky Hill Road was a stand of tall, planted pine trees with sedge grass growing in the sun underneath them. When Joe drove down the driveway, a covey of quail scooted across before scurrying into the tall grass. He didn't see any young ones in the covey, but it wouldn't be long now before new chicks would be hatching. The quail, always a good thing to see, had struggled to maintain their population with the loss of so many small farms in recent years. Small farms, with brushy fence rows, provided good habitat for them, while large cotton fields had little concealment to offer these birds. The hawks had almost wiped them out.

Belle leaped from the front porch when Joe arrived; she always greeted him before he could open the truck door with her wiggling butt and low friendly growls. Since his wife's death, Joe talked to the dog more than he did before. Perhaps a side effect of being alone, for amusement.

Joe leaned over, taking the dog's head in both hands, kneading her ears, "Hey, girl, you got breakfast ready? Why not? Ain't you worth nothing 'round here? Naw, you ain't, are you girl? That's a good girl."

He ascended the steps to the porch, "We gotta go in today and clean up for company, girl."

After a short rest, Joe prepared the house to welcome his company the next day. He swept the floors and wiped down the furniture, stretching fresh sheets on the beds. He checked the cupboards to make sure they held plenty of groceries, then brushed the cobwebs away from the ceiling of the front porch. Things Maggie always attended to when she ran the house.

After Joe finished the daily chores, he sat on the front porch swing to rest. He whistled like a bobwhite quail. One quickly whistled back. The view through the sparse trees beyond the front yard allowed him to tell if an occasional vehicle rumbled along Rocky Hill Road. He caught a glimpse of three kids. One rode a bicycle while the other two walked.

The Johnson's kids, he assumed, headed home from an after-school excursion. The Johnsons lived hand-to-mouth, like most folks around, but they were a good Christian family who lived just across the creek to the south of Joe's place, about a mile away. They had been the closest neighbors to Joe for the past twenty years. Fifteen years ago, the father, Aubrey, was disabled in a logging accident. Since then, the family had struggled to make ends meet. Being proud people, they didn't want charity— neighbors understood. However, Joe had visited often, always managing to offer whatever he had gathered from his garden or fruit from the orchard. More than once he had told Aubrey he'd killed a deer, only to notice he had no room in his freezer to store it. Under these guises, Joe managed to help feed the family, allowing Aubrey his pride.

Often, Joe would discover something around the house in need of repair, or a saw blade that required sharpening, taking it to Aubrey rather than doing it himself. This way, he was able to *pay* Aubrey for his work with some fresh eggs or tomatoes. The kids, well behaved, had always shown proper respect to their elders.

Dozens of families like this in Monroe County were scattered throughout the countryside, making a living the best they could, taking pride in their culture. That's why Joe loved it here. Family roots ran deep. His family went back for generations in Monroe County. The wildlife, woods and waters were a way of life to him. In addition, the rise of turkey populations in recent years served as icing on the cake.

His daughter had not felt the same deep connection to the community as her parents. She had dreamed of a different life, full of busy streets, tall buildings and bright lights. However, during her childhood, Nancy delighted in her father's attention, going on hunting and fishing trips with him often. She loved to help butcher the animals, especially deer. Nancy seemed fascinated by the internal organs, which she always wanted to feel and inspect.

Joe indulged her with enthusiasm. He relished having her with him in the garden, riding the tractor, while teaching her country life. As she grew older, however, she drifted away from those things, spending a lot of time reading, learning to cook and becoming a young woman. At times, Joe felt left behind but he had no idea how to relate to a teenage girl with her tender feelings. He feared he had lost connection with the little girl he loved so much.

She left for college at eighteen years old, where she met her soul mate. She married James McCoy the day after her graduation from Mobile College. They stayed in the city to pursue a better life, doing well, with good jobs in Mobile. Nancy became a bookkeeper while James worked as a real estate agent, eventually becoming a broker. They had a child in nineteen fifty-five. The boy, Connor. Joe and Maggie had visited them often, but the long trip in the old truck, all the way to Mobile, proved difficult. Recently, there were plans emerging for an interstate bridge all the way across the Tensaw Delta, which would reduce the travel time considerably.

Progress ... finally coming for south Alabama. Times are changing fast.

Joe noticed changes in his daughter since her husband's death. She asked about the people in the area more often. Perhaps she had developed a yearning for the simple, small-town life.

Joe missed his daughter, even after all these years. Her personality had always delighted him. When she moved away to college, Joe felt he had a hole in his heart. The feeling had returned since his wife passed.

The voices of the kids with the bicycle faded away, while even the bobwhite stopped calling. Joe meandered inside, ate supper, then sat by the fire with Belle.

Joe went to bed thinking about the Beatrice Farm, owned by his old friend Jessie Pickens. He planned to go there in the morning. His mind rambled through all the changes he'd seen take place over his sixty-seven years. He pondered the news reports about plans to have men go to the moon this summer. He pondered what changes his grandson, Connor, would experience in his lifetime.

CHAPTER 7 – A HAINT

Jessie Pickens was a wealthy man. He owned some of the best land in Monroe County. He had made his money in the timber business, working hard his whole life. Well-respected and fair, Jessie was a generous man. He remained a bachelor because he never met a girl who could keep up with his hard-working pace.

His farm, known as the Beatrice Farm, provided a paradise for a hunter. Much of the four-thousand acres contained longleaf pines along with mixed hardwoods. He scheduled different parcels of land for control-burning on a two-year rotation. Several creeks bordered the rolling hills throughout the place. Over three hundred Black Angus cattle grazed on hundreds of acres of prime pastureland scattered behind Jessie's home.

Joe became friends with Jessie early in Joe's career as a lineman. They connected the first day they met. Jessie had finished high school the previous year. Joe, only ten years older, was still a young man.

~~~~~~~

Joe was checking electric lines along the long, private road leading to Jessie's childhood home, when Jessie rode up one morning on a big black horse. During the conversation, one or the other raised the subject of wild turkeys.

Jessie's father once told him, "Never mess with wild turkeys, son, because they carry a 'haint.' In Jessie's story, somewhere in his father's past he had encountered a gobbler who had vanished into thin air, so Jessie never tried hunting these "supernatural" birds. In truth, an old, wise tom can slip behind a tree or clump of bushes then step straight away from a hunter's line of sight to obscure his escape. The hunter never sees the tom leave. If the hunter tends to be superstitious anyway, he will swear the gobbler vanished before his eyes. Joe had spoken to many negro loggers in the area, who tended to be even more superstitious than white folks, possessing a spooky view of gobblers because of these tales. It always amused Joe.

Joe knew better than to dispute the man's father. That would not be polite. He told Jessie he liked to hunt turkeys. Jessie became curious during the conversation, asking Joe to take him on a turkey hunt.

"I just gotta see what it's about," Jessie said.

Later that spring, Jessie Pickens, seventeen years old, against the good advice of his father, went on his first turkey hunt with Joe. He should have stayed home.

~~~~~~

It had rained heavily the day before they went, leaving the ground soaking wet. They carried along a few old magazines to sit on to keep their backsides dry. The air lay heavy with fog that morning when they arrived at the ridge, which ran along a wide creek-swamp below. They stood high on the ridge in the black dark, waiting on daylight, whispering to one another in the last minutes of night.

Jessie had grown into the quintessential country boy—burly, strong, with a shock of thick black hair. Even at seventeen, his beard would grow overnight. He stood six foot three inches tall, with muscles poking out from places Joe had never seen muscles grow. At the time, Joe didn't understand what deep fears resided inside Jessie's brain. The superstition had been implanted in him at a very young age by a father he trusted and idolized … but at seventeen years of age, a boy must find out things for himself. Jessie liked a challenge.

Jessie stood with Joe in the dark that morning with an invisible monkey on his back. So far, he'd done a good job of hiding it.

After a hint of daylight, Joe owled without warning Jessie. Not that he did that on purpose to shock Jessie, but he had simply forgotten to say anything before he did it.

This startled Jessie, as he flinched. "What'd you do that for? Dang it, man."

Joe apologized, explaining the purpose of the owl-call. Nothing answered.

They slinked along the ridge another hundred yards. Joe, making sure to warn Jessie first, owled again. This time the owl-call caused a tom to gobble farther along the ridge. They eased forward to a place that would locate them seventy-five yards uphill from the gobbler's location. Joe found a place with two trees growing close together and spread out the magazines to sit on beside one another with their backs against the trees.

"Put your gun on your knee and the stock against your shoulder, ready to shoot. Be real still," Joe whispered. "Don't move a muscle until you're ready to shoot, then shoot him in the neck when you do. I'm gonna try to call him to us."

"Okay," Jessie said, shifting into position.

Joe removed the box call from his vest, then gently stroked out four sweet hen-yelps followed by one cluck. The tom double-gobbled right back. The sound echoed through the quiet valley covered in the dim light. Joe lowered the call down to the ground, while shouldering his own gun. The tom continued to gobble from the roost's limb. Joe knew they had found a good one from the deep rattling sound of the turkey's voice. After ten minutes, the flapping of large wings signaled the tom flying down from the roost. The limb which had served as the roost cracked when he took off, which indicated to Joe a large, heavy bird. Too dark to put eyes on him, Joe sensed the tom's approach.

"Get ready," Joe whispered, cutting his gaze in Jessie's direction. Joe noticed the muzzle of Jessie's gun barrel upon turning his head; what he witnessed at that moment served as his first clue to Jessie's state of mind.

The gun barrel vibrated like the wings of a hummingbird—Jessie shook uncontrollably.

Joe could do nothing at this stage.

I'm gonna have to shoot this tom myself ... for dang sure.

Once the tom left the roost, he made no more sound. No gobbling. No drumming. Nothing. Minutes passed like hours. Joe strained to see any indication of the tom's movement toward them in the morning's dim light. The wet ground dampened any sound of footsteps. The whole forest slid into silence. Jessie's gun continued to quiver. Joe feared Jessie to be in terrible distress from trying to remain still.

After twenty long minutes of being stuck without the luxury to move, the next event became unbearable ... especially for poor ole Jessie. Not ten yards directly behind the two men, the loudest, most terrible, raspy gobble erupted. Jessie squealed like a girl as his entire two-hundred-thirty-pound body rose a foot from the ground. The gobble even startled Joe, who jerked aside. Jessie's gun fell from his hands to slap the ground in front of him. Jessie wheeled around to a position on his hands and knees as fast as he could, but no tom was in sight. The tom had fled on foot in a rush, after seeing the big man's startled reflex.

Jessie rolled onto his side, lying on the wet ground. "Oh, Lord, get me out-a-here!" Joe noticed that Jessie's eyes were wet. Somewhat embarrassed for this big, young man, Joe's heart sank examining Jessie, who had been brought to his knees by an unreasonable fear of a bird.

Joe tried to explain to Jessie what had happened. "That ole turkey snuck around behind us and we couldn't hear him coming because the ground's so wet."

"Oh, Lord, I ain't never messing with these turkeys again." Jessie huffed as he tried to calm himself down. "I ain't made for this kind of thing."

Jessie quickly rose to his knees, gazing at Joe, raising his eyebrows while canting his head aside, "You ain't gonna tell nobody about this, are you, Joe?" Jessie pleaded as he wiped his face.

Joe looked Jessie in the eyes, "I don't see that it's anybody's business, Jessie," Joe said. "Let's get on back to the house and get some food."

After that morning, Jessie never hunted turkeys again but his secret stayed between them. Joe never said a word to anyone about that morning at the Beatrice Farm. In addition, Jessie, learning Joe could be trusted as a friend, granted him permission to hunt the farm anytime he wanted, for as long as Jessie lived. Jessie kept his word, while the two men remained good friends throughout the years.

CHAPTER 8 – WALK AWAY

Connor jittered with excitement, knowing this day would be his last day at this school. No more bullies. No more fights. The future seemed brighter with the hope of a new life ahead of him. He couldn't wait for the day to end.

This being the first year many south Alabama schools were forced by the federal government to integrate white and black students, there were many tussles between the two groups. It seemed to Connor that the Negros wanted to attend even less than the whites wanted them attending. Most of the large battles, sometimes involving a dozen or more, occurred in the higher grades. The police patrolled the halls all day at school, putting everyone on edge.

At break times, large groups of Negro boys would gather together in one area while white kids did the same in another area. They may have been forced to attend the same school but they made certain not to socialize. Segregation was alive and well, just practiced on a smaller piece of real estate. Connor didn't get involved in the race riots. He had enough trouble with the white kids.

Connor stood tall and slender but solid, like a lighter'd knot, with lean, athletic grace. However, this phase of his growth drew unwanted attention from other boys, who in their adolescence sought what they perceived to be an easy target to "prove" their masculine superiority. Connor usually didn't have much to say, trying his best to ignore the bullies. However, when they crossed a certain line, Connor lost control, reacting with a fast, powerful right hook to the nose.

The anger he developed after losing his father had modified his threshold for letting things slide. It didn't take as much as it once did to trigger his rage; the boys who liked to scrap discovered they could provoke Connor at the drop of a hat.

To Connor, it felt good to fight. To direct his rage on a deserving opponent secretly served as a release.

His anger episodes had occurred three times in the past two months. He faced disciplinary action each time with a painful paddling in the principal's office. The last time, they sent him home for three days to face his mother. The disappointment expressed by her bothered him most. He would have rather received another paddling.

At lunch, Connor told someone that this would be his last day at the school. The word traveled fast. It wasn't long before some of the other boys began to taunt him. "So, you runnin' away? You too good for our school now?" The boys were relentless.

Connor's blood pressure began to rise.

One of the older boys kept this up so long that Connor finally had enough. But this time, he figured that since this was his last day anyway, he had a choice. He could stay, having to fight again, or he could simply head home. In nineteen sixty-nine, ditching school without permission was a serious violation. However, Connor decided it would be the best choice. After all, wasn't that what his parents had told him to do? "*Walk away, Connor*," they had said. "*Don't fight.*"

When the bell rang after lunch for the next class, Connor moseyed home, unseen by school officials. Walking the fourteen blocks to his house from the school, he took his time.

Once, a police car turned the corner ahead of him, rolling toward him along the street. Connor strolled onto the porch of the nearest house, as if he had arrived home. The police car passed without stopping to question his truancy. He made it home around two PM, four hours before his mom would arrive from work. Neither Connor nor his mother ever received any notice from the school. Of course, Connor never confessed what he'd done. Connor McCoy would never look back.

That night his mother helped him pack all his clothes, baseball equipment, and shotgun, along with most everything they could fit in the back of the station wagon. They left his bicycle. There was no room for it. The next morning, they would travel to Paw Paw's house. Connor could hardly sleep.

CHAPTER 9 – THE WAY OF THE SPIRIT

Joe awoke at three thirty Saturday morning and went through his morning routine before heading north up Hwy 21 to Beatrice. He planned to arrive at five AM at the farm, allowing time to have coffee with his old friend Jessie before the hunt. Jessie, always up by five AM, would be pleased to see Joe. The weather overnight had turned warm and dry, which eliminated any fog or heavy dew, making the hour-long drive to Beatrice pleasant.

When Joe climbed the steps to the front door, Jessie opened it before Joe had a chance to knock. "I figured that was you. Nobody else would come around here this early," Jessie laughed. "Come on in, coffee's ready."

The two men sat at the kitchen table catching up on the latest news of family news—marriages, deaths of friends—along with news about local boys returning from Viet Nam. Then the talk turned to turkeys. Joe inquired if Jessie had seen much activity this spring. Jessie reported sighting several large flocks around the property over the winter months but smaller groups this spring.

This was normal, Joe considered, because during the winter, large groups of hens travel together while groups of gobblers travel separately. When spring breeding season nears, the flocks peel off into smaller groups with toms gathering their harems of hens. Joe was pleased to hear that Jessie still had plenty of turkeys because Joe had not made the drive to Beatrice to scout before season.

"I seen something back in February that I ain't never seen here before, Joe," Jessie said. "It was a coyote. I swear it had to be a coyote. It weren't big enough to be no wolf. It looked sorta like a skinny, old, mangy dog ... but it weren't no dog."

"Well, I'll be. A farmer down in Little River seen one back during the winter. I reckon they're moving down here from the north," Joe replied.

"Well, if you see one, shoot it. I heard they will eat my calves."

"Will do."

Joe left, driving along a dirt road west of Jessie's house. Joe wanted to hunt this area because he'd hunted a very smart gobbler the season before but never killed him. He wanted to know if the same bird waited there this season.

After parking the truck, he hiked to a high hill to listen. The day had dawned already. Joe owled but got no response. When he hooted again, an owl far down in a hollow to the south answered but no gobbler sounded off. After several other tries, he strolled down the hill along an old road to another high spot about a half-mile away, to repeat the same routine.

When nothing answered his owling, he reached into his pocket, retrieving a crow-call. With several tries, only crows answered his call. He padded back to the truck to drive to another area farther north. At the next spot, he listened to hear several hens yelping as they gathered for their morning walk, but no gobblers made a sound.

Joe decided this was one of those mysterious mornings when gobblers do not speak.

Over the years, he had experienced hundreds of mornings when, no matter what, the gobblers would not gobble. Nobody knew why. One morning could be the exact same weather conditions as the morning before, when all the gobblers in the woods yelled at one another, but the next morning … not a peep.

Joe called to mind a Bible verse: "As you do not know the way of the spirit, nor how the bones grow in the womb of a woman with child, even so you do not know the work of God who maketh it all." Eccliastes. 11:5. Joe was convinced.

The Bible says some things cannot be understood by man. Why turkeys shut up on certain days must be one of those things.

After he had driven so far, Joe refused to quit. He decided to check a small pasture surrounded by low hills, resolving to be content to watch and wait. He found a good spot on the side of a hill offering him a clear view of the pasture below. He brought the thermos of coffee with him, figuring he would stay for a while to see what happened.

About halfway through his final cup of coffee, he spotted movement on the left side of the pasture. A doe emerged from the wood line to begin feeding on the green grass growing around the edges. Soon another deer appeared, feeding alongside. Before long, five does with a young buck grazed in the field.

A group of mischievous crows flew circles overhead, cawing loudly. They took turns flying low toward the deer, screaming caws the whole time. They continued diving toward the deer. Joe reckoned these crows were showing off to each other to see which one could harass the deer best.

Maybe they're "counting coup" like the Indians once did.

Occasionally, one of the younger deer lifted its head, tilted her ears back to stare at the crazy birds for a moment, then continued to graze. The crows caused no concern to her at all.

Gang mentality.

Joe watched the familiar scene he'd witnessed many times before. Crows would dive at a flock of turkeys, too. He supposed they found it entertaining.

The deer ate enough to satisfy their hunger before moving back into the safety of the woods. Near the other end of the pasture, he caught movement in the tall grass. Two hens strolled into the field, pecking the seeds at the top of the tallest strands of wheat while catching the bugs they disturbed. Before long, three other hens pecked their way near where the deer had been. Both groups of turkeys made a slow trek toward the middle of the pasture, joining together. Joe supposed these turkeys had been waiting for the crows to vacate before they ventured into the open field.

Two of the hens seemed to have a disagreement. One jumped in the air toward the other, causing her to run twenty yards away. Then both turkeys continued to peck at the ground as if nothing had happened between them.

To the right, something flickered. The motion occurred a hundred yards south along the edge of the wood line. He knew, from its size, it was a gobbler. The big bird glided along in full strut, its bright red color in the head and neck shone in the sun. The tom stepped slow and steady toward the flock of hens. When the tom got close to them, he stopped, turning from side to side so the ladies could be awed by all his wonderful iridescence. The hens seemed disinterested, but the tom never quit.

He strutted in the field for almost an hour until the hens were gone. He followed them into the forest edge where the entire flock faded into the timber. Joe considered hiking around in front of the flock of turkeys to try to call them. However, he had to beat it home before Nancy and Connor arrived. He decided since he had yet to hear a gobble, he would leave this group alone until another day. The hunt had been a success in Joe's view. Some hunts didn't need to include a dead turkey.

Joe could hardly believe his good luck this season already. The turkey population was certainly on the rise in this area. Times sure had changed since his younger days when just hearing a turkey gobble provided a rare treat. Joe reminisced on the old days during the drive back to Uriah.

How many things have changed ... some for the better.

Joe arrived home by nine-thirty AM, pouring a big glass of lemonade while he settled on the porch to wait. Belle lay at his feet, sleeping.

The Johnson kids walked along the road again. In the morning light he recognized the youngest child rode the bike while the other two marched alongside. Joe supposed they took turns riding the bike. He thought about calling to invite them to have a glass of lemonade but it was near time for his family to arrive.

Another time ... soon.

CHAPTER 10 - ARRIVAL

The yellow station wagon rolled along the driveway at ten-fifteen AM. Joe descended the steps to greet his family. Nancy's hugs were always lingering as kind words were spoken. The boy hugged his grandpa with a quick release.

Joe said, "How ya been, Connor?"

"I'm glad to be here," Connor knelt to pet Belle.

"Well, let's take all your luggage in and get you settled before lunch."

"I can only stay until tomorrow," Nancy said as they all carried suitcases up the steps of the porch.

Connor bounced up the steps, "Can we go hunting in the morning before church, Paw Paw?"

"We might manage a short hunt over at Jones Bluff if you're willing to do a few chores this week to pay me back," Joe said with a playful slap to Connor's head.

"All right, I can do that."

Nancy held the screen door open, "Daddy, I've arranged to take a vacation day next week to come back to get Connor registered in school after Spring Break. I'll drive up next Sunday. I just want to make sure he's settled in to the new school."

"That's a good plan, sweetheart. Me and Connor will spend the week working the spring garden. I'd like to get started on a few other things around here, too," Joe glanced at

Connor smiling. "We may even have to chase a few turkeys in our spare time."

"Yes, sir," Connor said as he raced to his room.

Joe turned to Nancy. "Meanwhile, this afternoon, I thought we could visit Maggie's grave, then take a drive over to Atmore to eat supper. Whatcha' think?"

"That sounds good," Nancy said.

Nancy volunteered to prepare lunch. After they placed Connor's things in one of the three bedrooms, they sat at the kitchen table to eat.

Joe patted Nancy's hand. "You making ends meet, sugar?"

"Yes, with James' life insurance, we're doing okay. And my job pays the bills. We're fine, Daddy."

"Good." He didn't want to pry but he worried about their finances. He worried most about their grief dealing with the loss of James. However, he wasn't sure how to broach the subject. He decided to let it go for now.

Glancing at Connor, Joe said, "How's that baseball career going, Connor? I hope you're planning to sign up here. They have a good team but I'm sure they would appreciate a good shortstop."

"Yes, sir. We'll see. I brought my glove and everything."

Joe loved baseball; he had played while a youngster. It pleased him that Connor had developed some real talent for the game early on. His wiry strength gave him the tools required to become a quick, nimble player. James had been a good teacher, having played for the college team.

"Spring practice should be started by now. You'll be just in time. Just remember, grades come first, baseball second."

Connor grinned. "Huntin' and fishin' second, baseball third, Paw Paw."

"Well, I reckon I can live with that," Joe said.

After lunch, Connor wandered outside while Joe and Nancy cleaned up the kitchen. He meandered around the yard, examining the oaks filled with tiny green buds on the limbs. The surrounding pines whispered in the breeze while Connor listened to the sounds of the countryside he loved. A distant crow cawed while various birds fluttered about the trees.

He drifted farther into the pines between the yard and the road. He picked up a long stick and began swinging it, slapping the tops of the sedge grass as he strolled. As he ventured near the road, enjoying the daydream-filled stroll, a covey of quail exploded in front of him, wings beating like drums. He jumped back, holding the stick in front of him for protection, then froze in surprise.

"Whoa," he said aloud before he could stop the words. His heart beat fast as he took a deep breath to calm down.

"You see them quail?" an unfamiliar voice said from the direction of the road.

Connor searched with squinted eyes through the trees to locate the source of the voice.

"One of 'em 'bout ran right into me," the young voice yelled as Connor realized it was speaking to him. Three faces beamed at him from the roadway. All he could see were their faces above the sedge grass where the roadbed dipped three feet below the level of Joe's land. A shallow ditch with a high bank of red dirt lined each side of the road. Connor approached the road, which revealed two boys and a girl. The girl straddled an old bicycle.

As Connor approached them his eyes locked on her face for a moment before he managed to speak, "Those quail just about scared the daylights outta me. I almost stepped on 'em."

One of the boys looked at least seventeen, the other much younger. They all laughed. Then the tallest boy said with a friendly voice, "You Mr. Joe's grandson, ain't ya."

"Yeah," Connor said.

"I'm Kenny," he said, then pointed toward the other boy. "That's my brother Clay and my sister Janice. What's your name?"

"Connor."

"How long you staying down here?"

"I think I'm moving here … What y'all doing out here?"

The younger boy, whom Connor assumed was around twelve years old, spoke with excitment, "We was going down to the creek to catch some crawdads an' just foolin' around. Wanna go?"

Then the girl spoke for the first time, "How old are you?"

"Fourteen. What about you?"

"I'll be fourteen soon," Janice said, smiling. Her smile caused Connor's stomach to turn over unlike anything he'd felt before. He could not remember receiving a smile like that from a girl back at his old school, especially a pretty girl.

Connor grimaced as his face turned red. His neck became hot suddenly. His heart fluttered as the words stumbled out, "Oh, that's cool." Recovering, he spoke to the group, "I don't think I can go with y'all today. Me and Paw Paw are going somewhere in a little while. How do y'all catch crawdads?"

"We can show you. Maybe in a couple days, if you're around," Kenny said.

The girl spoke again, "You gonna go to school in Uriah?"

"Yep, planning on it," he smiled at her.

Kenny looked at his sister, smirked and chuckled, "Well, we'll see ya later, Connor. We better get on down there. You watch out for them quail."

"Yeah, see y'all later," Connor said.

The girl raised her hand, waved with a cute smile, "Bye."

Connor managed to wave, but his voice wouldn't work anymore.

Connor turned toward the house, seeing that his mother and grandfather waited on the porch. As he approached, they both sat in the swing. Each held a cup of coffee. Connor relaxed as if he had been placed in paradise, the worry and stress that he had carried for the last several months slipping off his shoulders.

"Hey, Paw Paw, I almost stepped on a covey of quail," he said as he reached the edge of the front yard. "I 'bout had a heart attack."

Joe laughed as Nancy said, "They will make you hurt yourself. I used to see them when I was little ... so cute how they all scurry around together."

They finished the coffee, then piled into the yellow station wagon. Nancy drove to the cemetery where they replaced the old flowers in the concrete vase with some new black-eyed Susans Nancy had picked from the edge of the yard. Connor noticed the tombstone, made for two people to be buried beside one another. The other tombstone had no inscription.

Joe and Nancy used the drive to Atmore to catch up, reminiscing about family members. Connor wondered about the next morning's prospects for hunting turkeys.

~~~~~~~

As they passed in front of the state prison on Hwy 21, Connor, enthralled with the sight of men in white jumpsuits working in the vast fields around the prison, stared in amazement. Several men on horses, with shotguns in their hands, rode alongside the lines of working prisoners.

Connor mulled over what they could have done to end up there. His imagination soared as they passed the high fences around the prison with the barbed wire stretched along the top. Joe had told him this was where they kept the electric chair to put the worst criminals to death. A chill ran along Connor's spine, causing him to shiver.

When they arrived at Albert's Restaurant, all thoughts of the prison had faded. He relaxed to enjoy spaghetti with meatballs.

"I'm looking forward to church tomorrow," Nancy said as they were leaving. "It will be good to see everyone again."

"Well, ain't much changed there." Joe said. "A few less old people that have passed on. A few kids sprouting up. Not a lot of people anxious to move up here I guess."

"Still, I like it there, it always feels like home."

CHAPTER 11 – SEEING TOO WELL

Sunday morning came warm and muggy. When they left the house, Connor brought his twenty-gauge single-shot. The Stevens shotgun was given to him for Christmas two years back. He'd used it to kill his first turkey while sitting between Joe's knees on a windy, rainy morning the very next spring.

Connor, excited about the hunt, was close to over-stimulation. Paw Paw had offered him a cup of coffee with sugar. Connor took advantage of the rare treat, most often offered only to adults.

Jones Bluff was only four miles away. The drive was short. Joe gave Connor his usual reminders about being still and always keeping the gun pointed in a safe direction while the pickup rattled along to the hunting ground.

Connor locked the gate behind the truck; they waited in the cab while whispering their final thoughts before daylight signaled time to go listen for turkeys. As the first light brightened the sky, they padded down an old trail to the top of Jones Bluff. This high ridge afforded a listening post to the wide, flat creek-swamp wrapped around three sides of the north-facing bluff. They stood in the dawn, waiting for the cardinal's call.

"Never call before the first cardinal chirps," Joe had said.

Connor remembered.

~~~~~~~

Joe hadn't scouted the area prior to the season opening, but he knew that in this place either you heard one or you didn't. There wasn't much use in scouting. He knew the terrain. He'd hunted here for many years. It usually held a small group of turkeys with at least one gobbler each season.

Jones Bluff offered only two hundred acres of land on this side of the big creek, so there was a limit to how far a man could go after a turkey without trespassing. Joe hadn't killed one here in four years. They would listen first from this elevated position, then go to the turkey once a gobble was heard.

However, even after the sky lightened and the cardinals sang, no turkey was heard. An owl hooted far down in the hollow to the east. Later, nearby crows started calling but still no gobbling. Joe questioned if this may be a repeat of yesterday's "no gobbling" day. Tired of waiting, Joe decided an owl-call might produce results. He owled several times before the faint sound of a gobble drifted from the west, low in the creek-swamp.

"Let's slip lower toward the creek and see if we can get closer," Joe whispered. They eased down the hill toward the gobbler.

When they reached the creek bottom, they stopped to listen again. Nothing. Joe owled again. The tom answered before he finished; the sound still two hundred yards away.

"Easy now," Joe whispered as they maneuvered closer. Joe scanned for a good place to set up.

When they were within one hundred yards from the gobbler, Joe said, "We better stop here. It's getting light. He might see us if we go any farther. There's a good tree to sit and lean back on over there. You sit there and I'll sit by this one to your left and a little farther back. We'll be close enough to hear each other whisper."

After they settled into their spots, they listened again for several minutes but heard nothing. Then Joe used the box call to make two clucks. The turkey gobbled again but only once.

This turkey ain't excited at all.

Joe waited fifteen minutes without another gobble. He used the call to make four short, sweet yelps. The turkey gobbled again. He had flown away from his roost tree downhill toward the creek to their right.

He's going to get some water.

Joe had experienced this before. A turkey would gobble a little, fly from his roost, then head straight for the nearest water source, as if he were so thirsty he couldn't gobble much. Joe also knew, from experience, after they drank their water, they would sometimes come to a call, gobbling all the way.

Knowing the location of the gobbler, Joe took the opportunity to whisper to the boy, "He's gone to get a drink. Be patient. We still got a chance."

Joe gave the turkey another ten minutes, then called with the same lonesome hen yelps. The tom responded quickly from farther along the bottomland to the right. From the sound, Joe figured the turkey was standing by the creek. Joe flicked the lid of the box call, making a cluck, this time a little louder than before. Another gobble. Joe could tell it had come closer.

Joe whispered, "Slide around your tree and face toward the turkey."

Connor, being as quiet as he could, slid around and got his knees back up in front of him before placing the forearm of the shotgun on his kneecap. He snugged the butt of the stock against his shoulder.

Joe waited with his head turned in the direction of the last gobble while scouting for movement beneath the trees. The tom gobbled without provocation from seventy yards away. Joe and Connor saw it at the same instance. The tom's red and blue

56

head glinted slightly to their left. Joe watched it appear and disappear through the woods, continuing left. Then it turned to take a few steps to the right. The tom gobbled again. Back and forth he went.

Joe held the call in his lap with both hands, hidden from the direction of the gobbler's keen eyes. He pulled the lid slowly across the box to make a purr.

The tom stopped, raised his head high, peering in their direction. He double-gobbled, making two gobbles back to back, so close together, it sounded like one. The tom lifted his tail feathers, making a fan. He went into full strut, puffing all his feathers outward around him. Continuing his back and forth mating display, he moved with graceful steps, floating left to right, right to left.

They watched the tom for thirty minutes. Now and then, Joe carefully reached down, scratching the leaves on the ground to mimic a feeding hen. One scrape across the leaves, a pause, and then two more. Every time he did it, the turkey would gobble.

When a tom decides he ain't coming any closer without seeing a hen, there's not much you can do except wait.

Ten more minutes passed. The tom ceased gobbling and strutting as he drifted away. Joe did not call again. It was time to go. Church began in an hour and a half. He knew this tom could be hunted again. He waited for the tom to go far enough away so their movements would not be seen.

Joe whispered, "Let's go. He'll be here another day."

As they hiked to the truck, Connor whispered, "He hung up, didn't he Paw Paw?"

"Yep, he hung up for sure. I think he could see too well."

"Wha'cha mean, see too well?"

"Well, if you set up in a place where the woods are so open and clear that the turkey can see a long way, that's a bad situation sometimes. That turkey knew exactly where my calls were coming from, but when he looked in that direction, he didn't see a hen. That makes him suspicious and he'll hang up until a hen shows herself. He knows that if he gobbles and struts long enough, the hen is supposed to come to him where he can see her. Until then, he doesn't trust the situation. It's better to set up in a place where the tom has to get close to see the area that the hen sound came from. That way, you can get 'em into gun range. This gobbler was too smart for us today. We set up in the only location we could find, but I figure this tom is older and he just outsmarted us. Next time, we'll set up in a better position."

"Durn ole turkey," Connor muttered.

Joe laughed. "Well, that's a good name for him. Durn Ole Turkey. Hmm, seems to fit."

"He deserves a dang stupid name," Connor grumbled. "Maybe we can make a fake turkey hen and stick it up in front of us. He'll see it next time and come to us."

Joe stopped walking. He turned to face Connor, putting his hand on his hip, "Why don't we just go down to Joe Hadley's place and buy one of his farm turkeys, take it home, tie it to a tree in the back yard and shoot it in the head? I'd get the same satisfaction from that as I would from your idea."

Connor lowered his head, "Yeah, that was dumb."

"Don't let the desire to kill ruin your desire to hunt, son."

"Yes, sir."

"Connor, you done real good. You sat there for over an hour and didn't move. You're becoming a good hunter, son. I'm proud of you."

Connor's heart swelled with pride as his lips tightened into a wide grin. He smiled up at his grandfather, "My butt went to sleep," he said, laughing.

"Yep, I know what you mean, son … happens to me more and more often lately." Joe chuckled and patted the boy's shoulder.

CHAPTER 12 - REVELATIONS

Back at Joe's house, Nancy had sausage biscuits warming in the oven. After a quick change of clothes, followed by breakfast, they rode to church in the station wagon.

The thought of being a stranger in Sunday school turned Connor's stomach into a queasy mess. He took some comfort in the fact that on previous visits there, he'd found most people were kind and friendly.

Sunday school commenced at ten AM. A deacon led Connor to the class for teens. When he entered the room, the girl he had seen on the road the day before sat inside; she wore a bright blue dress. Today, the girl seemed different. Her hair shone like the color of dry wheat in the sun and her skin gleamed as if oiled, leading Connor to think it glowed. He felt his heart flutter when the girl locked eyes with him and said, "Hey."

"Hey," Connor said, sitting in the only empty chair in the room, right beside her. The teacher introduced the other seven kids to Connor. To his surprise, the teacher already knew Connor's name. Connor listened little to what the teacher said during the lesson. For most of the next forty-five minutes, he stared at the lesson book they had given him while his mind raced to uncover answers to two burning questions: how to talk to this girl and what to say.

Connor didn't have to think of anything, however, because as soon as the closing prayer ended with the teacher saying

"Amen," Janice faced him. "So, is Mr. Joe keeping you busy today?"

"Yeah, I guess so; we went turkey hunting this morning. It was so cool," Connor said.

"Cool, huh?" She giggled. "What happened?"

Connor told her the whole chain of events as they strolled outside under the big live oaks in the churchyard. She seemed genuinely interested, which caused Connor to relax.

Then, later in the conversation, he decided to make one of the boldest moves of his life. As he gathered his courage, putting both hands in his pants pockets while swaying back and forth gazing directly down at his feet, he said, "Will you sit with me during church service?"

Janice lowered her head and didn't say anything for a moment. Then, she returned her gaze to Connor, with an apologetic face, "I have to ask my mom."

Connor felt his face fill with blood, "Oh ... sure, I understand. I'll save you a spot in case she says yes." Connor quickly responded.

Janice smiled, cocked her head shyly to one side and nodded.

They passed through the doors of the sanctuary, seeking their respective families, who were already seated.

Connor sat by his mom, with Joe, on the sixth row. He hoped the cold, hard, pews didn't forecast Janice's parents reaction to his bold request. The piano played as people filtered into the bleak, sterile sanctuary.

The music stopped playing as the preacher rose to welcome everyone. Connor realized she wasn't coming to sit with him. He resisted the urge to turn his head to scan the crowd for her. Thoughts of doom rattled around in his head. He sat, ruminating about what her mother might have said.

Have I been too bold? After all, fourteen years old might be too young to sit with a girl in church in Uriah, Alabama.

Back in Mobile, kids my age had girlfriends right out in the open. I knew things were different here. I should have asked her about that. I just met her. What kind of dumb move was that?

Oblivious to the opening of the services, obsessing about his mistake, Connor's head jerked when the preacher called his name. He panicked. His face flushed. Since he'd been daydreaming instead of listening to the preacher, he had no idea why the preacher said his name. He froze. Several parishioners called "Amen."

What was going on?

Then the preacher finished his sentence, "… and we welcome all our *other* visitors this morning to the house of the Lord."

Connor's heart continued racing as the crowd stood to sing the first hymn. He gulped five deep breaths to calm himself down as the open hymnal in his hands shook and the congregation sang. "Praise the Lord, praise the Lord, let the earth hear His voice."

Sometime during the third verse, he regained his normal breathing … and for that, Connor McCoy praised the Lord.

After church, the people filed out the front door, each one with a customary handshake with the preacher waiting just outside. Joe and Nancy shook hands with many of the folks standing in the churchyard. Everyone seemed glad to see Nancy again, while some made a fuss about how tall Connor had grown.

A man and woman approached to shake Joe's hand, exchanging greetings. Beside them, Janice stood, smiling at Connor.

"Well, Joe, I want to meet this young man you have here," the woman said.

As Joe introduced Connor to Janice's parents, she said, "I hear you're gonna be living in Uriah with your grandpa and going to school with Janice here."

"Yes, ma'am," Connor said.

"Well, why don't you come over to our house after lunch? We're making some homemade ice cream. You like ice cream, Connor?"

"Yes, ma'am," Connor said, his heart racing

"And Joe, you and Nancy are welcome, too."

Joe glanced at Nancy, who nodded.

"That sounds mighty fine, Velma. Thank you, we'll be glad to come," Joe said.

Joe took only a second to recognize what just happened.

Connor and the young Miss Janice Johnson have taken an interest in one another. Somehow, her mama has caught on.

Joe knew it would be proper for the girl's parents to have an opportunity to get to know the boy before they would allow any further development. He was happy to accommodate for the sake of his grandson, but wondered how this had developed right under his nose since yesterday. The thought of it amused him.

My goodness, I'm not only old, I'm slow, too.

On the way home, Joe teased the boy.

"Well, well, Connor, you sure do move quick," Joe said.

"Daddy," Nancy said, "don't tease Connor. He's old enough to like girls. She sure is cute."

Joe glanced into the backseat, watching Connor who had reddened.

"So, tell me about it, Connor. Did you just meet her this morning?"

"No, sir. She was with her brothers on the road yesterday, right after I flushed those quail. I met them there."

"I see. Well, I'm glad we're getting some homemade ice cream outta' this deal anyway," Joe said as he turned and winked at Nancy.

"Daddy! Now, you quit," Nancy said, playfully slapping Joe's shoulder.

~~~~~~~

Nancy's excitement for her son was hard to conceal.
He's going to be fine ... just fine.
She tried to assure herself.

She cooked fried strips of wild turkey breast with mashed potatoes for Sunday dinner, while Joe and Connor went for a stroll to the back pasture. Joe whistled the bobwhite call. Toward the west, a response came from a male right away.

"That's a male, Connor. Just two notes ... bobwhite, bobwhite. The females call with three notes," Joe said.

Connor smiled, "I *remember,* Paw Paw."

"Well, okay then."

The sun became hot as they passed alongside the chicken house. Joe noticed a hole had been dug under the fence. He knelt to inspect the dirt in the bottom of the hole.

"Another fox," he said. "I'm gonna have to handle this before dark. He prob'ly got a chicken last night. We'll have to catch that fox, son."

The chickens, more than fifteen of them, were released from the pen during most days to forage the land. Each late afternoon, just before dark, the chickens would wander into the pen to roost for the night. Joe would close the gate to the pen to protect them.

Occasionally, a fox, raccoon or chicken snake would locate a way inside to help itself to a meal. A constant battle, Joe knew he'd have to deal with the fox soon. They were smarter than the raccoons, which made them harder to catch.

"How are you going to catch that fox?" Connor asked.

"We'll come back down here late this afternoon when we get back and I'll show you," Joe said. "Let's go eat. I don't want to keep your young lady waiting too long."

"Aw, Paw Paw," Connor said. They headed toward the house.

On the way, Connor grilled Joe with several questions about the Johnson family to see what Joe knew about them.

"Janice is nice," Connor said. "And pretty."

"I'd say so." He put his hand on Connor's head, ruffling his hair. "I'd say so."

Joe always said grace before each meal at home. Always the same prayer. "Heavenly Father, we thank Thee for these and all the other blessings we receive, amen."

Connor had memorized it.

While Joe's family enjoyed the fried turkey breast dinner, the conversation turned to Connor's situation with school.

"Connor has a problem with his temper, Daddy," Nancy said.

"I just get too mad sometimes," Connor replied.

Joe looked at Connor, "Let me ask you a serious question. Do you feel kinda' nervous, embarrassed, or shy a lot?"

Connor dropped his head, "Yes, sir, everybody at that school thinks I'm stupid except the baseball team. I get along with them fine."

Joe put his fork and knife on the table. He propped his arms on the edge of the table, examining Connor. "Son, I'm gonna tell you something man to man. And maybe only a man can really understand what I'm about to say. It's a secret that most all men over the age of twenty-five know. It takes about that long to realize it, and most fourteen-year-old boys have never been told what I'm about to tell you. So, listen close, I'm gonna tell you the truth about something."

"Yes, sir." Connor, unconsciously mimicking his grandpa, placed his fork on the table to listen.

"Every boy that gets up around thirteen or fourteen feels unsure of himself. They feel ugly, gangly, and stupid; they lose all their self-confidence with social situations. It's natural. But remember, you're not the only one."

Joe cocked his head, "Now, most of these boys try to *hide* it. They cover for it … in lots of different ways. Some become bullies because they think that will make them feel better. Some will act snooty because that's the only way they can deal with it. Some will be constantly sarcastic and criticize everything."

Joe held up two fingers, "There are two things that you have to remind yourself of every day. Number one is you ain't the only one your age who feels the way you do. You ain't alone.

"Number two is … it ain't your fault. It's nature, it's part of growing into a man. It ain't fair, and it ain't easy, but it don't last forever.

"You just gotta' remind yourself of that every day. Just hang tough. It'll pass. It's one of the hardest times you'll go through in your whole life. After you survive it, you will become stronger."

Connor took it all in. He'd never heard his Paw Paw talk this way. He felt special. His grandfather had shared a secret.

Connor noticed his mother's startled reaction as she said, "Daddy, I never realized that it could be so severe for young boys. I think that's good advice. Don't you, Connor?"

"You mean everybody my age feels the same?"

"I guarantee it, son. Some go through it earlier than others, but it happens to every boy … if they're normal."

Connor resumed eating while Joe and Nancy talked of other things. He considered what he'd heard.

Maybe Paw Paw's right. Hmm .... Paw Paw knows more than he lets on.

CHAPTER 13 – THE CHURNING

They drove the mile to the Johnson's home. The washboard road caused the Falcon station wagon to rattle as they drove, threatening to fall to pieces. A cloud of red dust rose behind them but quickly dissipated in the southern breeze.

As they pulled in the driveway, they noticed the dogwoods blooming under the pines along the edge of the yard. Purple azaleas bloomed on huge bushes.

Connor noticed the bicycle, settled on its side near the front steps. A large assortment of old, rusty farm equipment lay scattered along the yard's edge but there was no trash visible.

As Nancy switched off the ignition, Mr. Johnson opened the screen door and stepped onto the porch. He wore a white short-sleeved shirt with blue denim overalls. A large man, he stood tall and straight. "Y'all come on in. The boys are breaking ice on the back porch. Everything's ready to get this batch of ice cream started," he said in a booming voice.

Small talk between the adults ensued as Connor took a seat on the swing while the adults went inside.

Janice came outside smiling. "You wanna go around back with us? Kenny's got a big ole hammer banging on a block of ice. Ya gotta bust it up so it'll fit around the ice cream freezer."

"Sure." He followed Janice around the house to the backyard. Kenny stood over an old table with a big galvanized washtub on it. A block of ice slipped around inside. He chipped at the block.

Kenny paused, observing Connor, "Hey, Connor. You wanna bang on this for a minute? My arm's getting tired."

Clay, the younger brother, ran toward them, "One big ol' piece of ice flew off awhile ago and drilled Kenny right in the face." He yelled while flailing his arms to emphasize the flight of the ice chip. He bent over, put his hands on his knees and laughed, before running to a nearby tree to jump and cling to a low limb.

"Dang. That could hurt," Connor said, taking the hammer from Kenny.

Connor spotted a catcher's mitt cradling a dirty baseball lying on the table near the tub. "You play ball?" he inquired as he began smashing the block of ice.

"Yeah, I'm the catcher. Been the catcher since the tenth grade. I'm a senior this year. You play?"

"Shortstop mostly, but I pitch some, too." Connor swung the hammer.

"Huh. Maybe you can try out for the team," Kenny said.

Connor swung the hammer again, "Hope so."

~~~~~~

Janice watched and listened. She noticed the muscles in Connor's lean arms as he hammered at the ice.

He's cute and nice ... and he can play ball, too?

After they reduced the block of ice to a tub of watery chunks, the boys carried it around to the front porch. Mrs. Johnson had assembled the freezer on the porch. She placed the stainless-steel cylinder in the middle of the wooden pail, then connected a device with a big crank on top of the cylinder. She filled the space around the cylinder inside the wooden pail with ice, sprinkling some rock salt from a box on the floor before wrapping a thick towel around the top. "Y'all get to crankin'," she said with a smile toward Kenny.

The three boys took turns cranking the ice cream maker. At times the ice would jam, making the cranking difficult for a turn or two. Everyone else stood around the porch talking while the boys churned ice cream.

As the cranking became harder, after several pauses to add more ice, Mr. Johnson announced the decision, "It's ready."

After the lid of the cylinder and the paddles inside were removed, the cold ice cream was served to everyone. Connor and Janice took a seat on the swing.

Clay, sitting on the steps of the porch, screamed, "Oh, my face!"

He was holding his head in both hands. Kenny said, "Brain freeze," and laughed.

Mrs. Johnson scolded Clay, "Don't eat so fast and that won't happen."

Everyone chuckled.

"You gonna register for school next Monday then?" Janice asked Connor.

"Yep. What's it like there? Is there anything I need to know?" Connor said.

Janice explained the layout of the school, talking about a few of the teachers. "Mrs. Harris is the meanest teacher in the school. She teaches English. Coach Davis teaches history and coaches baseball. He's cool. It's okay there. Most of the kids are nice. Hardly anything new ever happens. I've known all the white kids since I was little. The colored kids just came here this year, but they seem nice."

They talked about sports, music and what it was like living in Mobile. They talked so much that before Connor realized it, Joe announced, "We better get back home. I've got to set a trap for a fox before it's dark." Joe shook Mr. Johnson's hand while everyone said their goodbyes.

Mrs. Johnson turned to Connor, "How'd you like that cream?"

"It was really good. Thank you, ma'am."

"Well, maybe you won't be a stranger around here. You just come visit anytime."

Connor stammered. "Yes, ma'am, I will … and thank you."

~~~~~~

Driving home, his mom said, "Well, you must have passed the test, Connor."

"Yes, ma'am," Connor said. He watched through the window as they passed the dogwoods in the afternoon shade of the pines, sparkling like tiny lights, twinkling in the shaded woods.

When they arrived home, Joe told Connor to follow him to the barn. Joe removed a trap that hung on the wall inside. On the way out, he picked up a shovel. They went to the chicken pen where they found most of the chickens already inside. Joe scraped the hole a little deeper, placed the trap in the bottom and attached its chain to a nearby post. As he worked, Joe explained each step to Connor. After covering it with loose soil, he backed away to survey the scene.

Hopefully, the fox would go through the same hole made the night before. The trap would spring, holding him there until morning. That was the plan.

Connor had been attentive. He enjoyed learning the skills his grandpa taught him. He could hardly wait until morning to check the trap. He'd never seen a live fox up close.

~~~~~~

Nancy waited for them on the back porch to say her goodbyes. As she hugged them both tight, she said, "Connor, you be good for Paw Paw this week, and I'll be back next Sunday."

When Nancy pulled onto Rocky Hill Road, tears welled up in her eyes. *Life changes,* she thought. However, something was changing inside her, too.

~~~~~~~

That night, they made their plans for the next morning's hunt. After they checked the trap, while it was still dark, they would head for the Thompson Tract.

"We don't want to leave a live animal in the trap any longer than we have to. So, we'll go out there before we go hunting to check it," Joe said.

As Connor nestled in bed that night thinking about the fox, he thought how lucky he was to be here.

CHAPTER 14 – NECESSARY KILL

Joe began filling his thermos with coffee when Connor came into the kitchen, rubbing his eyes, yawning.

"I think we might'a caught a fox," Joe said.

Connor's eyes widened, "How do you know, Paw Paw?"

"Cause I ain't heard that rooster yet. Usually by this time, he's already crowing. Now, if a live fox is down there, that ole rooster ain't gonna say a word to give away his location. He always roosts just outside the pen in those tall bushes to the right side."

Connor grabbed a glass of water, downed it, then poured a glass of milk. Sitting at the table with Joe, he ate one of the leftover biscuits from Sunday dinner. A light snack before the hunt was the routine. Breakfast would come later.

When they finished the snack, Joe got a big flashlight from the top of the refrigerator while heading for the backdoor with Connor following behind. Joe paused a moment on the back porch, grabbing an old, broken, three-foot-long hoe handle before descending the steps with Belle at his side.

When they neared the pen, the first thing Connor noticed was a low growling sound. Belle began to bark. When the beam of the flashlight found the spot where they had set the trap, a large red fox stared straight into the light.

Joe spoke to Belle, "Back."

Belle settled in a sitting position but Connor could see her restless posture. Her body was quivering with excitement. Connor realized he was shaking, too.

"Whoa. He's big," Connor said.

Joe eased close to the frightened animal, swung the hoe handle, popping the fox on top of its head. The fox went limp. Joe waited a moment then poked the fox's head with the end of the hoe handle.

"He's gone," Joe said quietly.

Connor detected sadness in the old man's voice.

Joe removed the fox from the trap, hoisted the body by its bushy tail, and handed him to the boy.

"Let's take him to the house to hang him on the porch until we get back. Then we can skin and stretch the hide."

"Yes, sir." He admired its beautiful coat. "His coat is thick."

"Yep, he hasn't lost his winter coat yet. He'll make a fine skin," Joe said as they turned toward the house.

Connor knew killing the fox was necessary. The chickens had to be protected, but part of him felt sorry for the big red fox. As he slid his hand across the fur, he wondered if the sadness he felt was normal or if he was different.

Chapter 15 - Home

When they arrived at the Thompson Tract, a light rain had passed through the area. Joe switched the engine off, he "We may end up with some soggy bottoms this morning, buddy. Might ought to take some of those newspapers behind the seat with us to sit on."

Connor opened the door. "Okay, I'll get 'em."

They made their way to the back of the pasture heading toward the burned area where Joe had encountered the turkeys Friday morning.

Joe pointed to the west. "If them hens are roosted in the same place they were Friday, we need to get over that way. Maybe we'll be in-between the gobblers and the hens," he whispered before stepping carefully in that direction.

They found a suitable place to set up as daylight filtered through the cloudy sky. Joe snipped several bushes to build a blind for them to sit behind and removed two shotgun shells from his pocket before reminding Connor to load his gun. They dropped the newspapers on the damp ground in each of their sitting spots, settling in to wait and listen for the woods to wake up.

He whispered again to Connor, "If there's more than one, shoot the strutter if you can."

"Yes, sir, I know." Connor whispered without turning his head.

This boy remembers a lot of what I taught him. He's about ready to try this on his own.

When the dawn came, Joe owled. A tom turkey gobbled two-hundred yards in front of them, down in the creek bottom. Joe waited for a few minutes before using the cedar box to make a single loud cluck, followed by a soft three-note yelp. The tom answered right away. Joe gazed in the direction of the gobble.

Now where's your two buddies this morning?

Joe put the box call down while he sliced his eyes toward Connor. Connor held his position with his gun's forearm resting on his left knee. Its stock firmly against his shoulder and the barrel pointed in the general direction of the turkey's voice, Connor was breathing heavy. His face was an inch from the stock with both eyes open, searching for movement. He was ready.

The tom gobbled on his own twelve more times from the same location. Then, after a fifteen-minute wait, Joe cupped the call to send another series of yelps.

When the tom gobbled again, he was on the ground and had closed the distance by half. Joe put the call on the dry newspaper under his raised knee and cradled his shotgun against his cheek, waiting.

The land in front of their position had a slight drop as it fell away to the creek bottom. Joe caught movement about ninety yards out. A bright red ball floated through the landscape, then another. A third red head materialized behind the first two. All three gobblers had flown from their roost, emerging together as they ambled toward Joe's call.

Connor's heart thumped so hard he was afraid the turkeys might hear it.

In a slow hunt-and-peck way, the three gobblers moseyed along the incline toward them. When the toms came within sixty yards, Joe cut his eyes toward Connor and assessed the situation.

"Cock the hammer," he whispered.

Connor's gloved thumb slid to the hammer's tang as he cocked it slow, so as not to make a sound. He eased his thumb back into position, wrapping it around the stock of the gun, while laying his trigger finger alongside the trigger guard. The three toms kept coming. The gobbler in the front went into a full strut and paused, gobbled, then resumed his slow progress forward.

The two toms following the boss were pecking and moving from side to side. All three were standing side by side, separated by five yards, only twenty-five yards in front of Connor when he pulled the trigger.

The strutter rolled to one side, flapping his powerful wings while lying on his side. The other two birds took to the air, big wings disturbing the damp morning air with each mighty stroke. Connor quickly broke the action of the gun, ejecting the spent shell, inserting another before pointing the gun at the bird.

"Don't shoot. Go get him," Joe said, "He's yours now."

Connor sprinted to the downed bird and pressed his boot on the turkey's neck, until the flopping subsided.

By that time, Joe had gathered his call and the newspaper. He approached the dead bird and slapped Connor's back, "Good shot, son."

Connor was shaking. He heart was beating as if his chest would burst open. He knelt to examine the sharp spurs, at least an inch long, with a slight curve in each one. The spurs were the best indication of the tom's age. The wide beard would measure more than ten inches long. The bird was at least three years old, maybe four.

"That's a fine one, Connor. I bet he'll weigh eighteen pounds," Joe said.

They lingered, admiring the bird, talking about what happened. After fifteen minutes, Connor's shaking had subsided. He hoisted the bird by its legs, slung it over his shoulder and carried it back to the truck.

After Connor loaded the turkey in the bed of the truck, Joe poured a hot cup of coffee from the thermos. "This has been the best season I've had in a long time. We had a good hatch two years ago, and I've seen more turkeys this year than I've ever seen before," he said.

"That's good, Paw Paw. You've been waiting a long time for a season like this."

Joe squinted his eyes. "Yeah, I reckon the wild turkeys have made a comeback from the old days. I used to have to hunt for two weeks just to hear one gobble. It was real tough. Reckon that's why very few men hunted them back then." He chuckled, "There ain't many that hunt them now, but if they keep coming back, the hunters will catch on sooner or later; then we'll have more competition."

When they returned home, Joe said, "Whew, we've got a lot of work to do before we start on the day's regular chores, son."

They cleaned the turkey first, placing the breast and thighs in waxed paper for freezing. Joe put the legs and beard upside down in a mason jar with some borax in the bottom to cover the exposed meat, curing it. They tacked the fan flat, in the open position, on a plywood board before pouring more borax on its meaty base.

The fox was skinned from its tail to the tip of its nose. It took Joe an hour of delicate knife work to do it. He stretched the skin over a smooth board. He then began to flesh the hide with an old piece of lawn mower blade he had sharpened, with handles on both ends for scraping hides. The blade, made from tempered steel, held an edge, while being wide enough to use both hands to scrape the hide clean.

Joe saw Connor's face grimace while watching the fleshing process. Joe was an old hand at this messy job, but he insisted that Connor pitch in to learn. They took turns scraping the leftover fat and flesh from the inner side of the hide with the blade.

When they finished with the fox, salting it to dry, they had worked up a healthy appetite. Joe said, "Let's go up to the restaurant and get some breakfast today."

"I'm ready for that Paw Paw. I'm *starving.*"

The meal was devoured. Fresh coffee followed. Although it was after ten AM, four of the farmers sat in the diner talking shop. All of them spoke to Joe, taking time to congratulate Connor on his gobbler.

As the famers talked, today's big news revolved around Mrs. Baker, the beloved office manager for Pickens Timber Company. She had announced, at the Methodist Church yesterday, she would retire this year. Mrs. Baker had been with Jessie Pickens's company for thirty years, dealing with all the loggers, suppliers, and buyers at the lumber mills. She was important to many people in Monroe County. Jessie, especially, had depended on her skills in helping his business remain stable, even through the last years of the Great Depression.

After arriving home, they picked a bushel of turnip greens, filling a grocery sack for the Johnsons. The remainder would become their supper, along with cornbread and bacon.

Connor and Joe worked side by side, while he told Joe more details about his year at school, the troubles he'd had, and talked about the baseball team.

The coach had awarded the starting shortstop position to him, an honor usually reserved for juniors or seniors. However, the coach thought him more capable than the other shortstop, who had been relocated to play second base. The coach helped develop his pitching, too. Connor enjoyed practices except for running the bleachers.

A few weeks remained before baseball season would begin. The coach was not going to be happy to learn Connor had left the school. This was the only regret Connor could think of.

Connor switched the conversation to turkeys. "What do wild turkeys do in the rain?"

"They either stay in the trees or they get in the middle of an open field and stay there. Both places are safe for them. When it rains, all the leaves and bushes in the woods are moving because the rain is beating on them.

"Turkeys can't spot the movement of bobcats when the woods are moving with the rain or if it's really windy. So, they go out in an open field where they can see for a distance all around them. And, the bigger the flock, the safer they are, more eyes to watch out for danger. Sometimes they just stay up in the trees where they're safe, but there ain't much to eat up in a tree, so they usually come down in the fields.

A wild turkey has to worry about predators even when they are still in the egg. Raccoons, blue jays, snakes, crows, 'possums and lots of other animals eat the eggs when they find 'em. When they're little, the mama hen watches for hawks and bobcats. And now, we're starting to see coyotes around here. I'm sure they can catch and eat a full-grown gobbler."

"Who taught you about all this stuff, Paw Paw?"

"I reckon I learned it mostly from being in the woods and noticing things. My daddy didn't hunt turkeys. I only knew one other turkey hunter when I was young. He was real stingy about it and didn't want to help nobody. So, I guess I learned it the hard way. Trial and error."

"Man, I'm glad you're teaching me."

"The best way to learn sometimes is to make a plan and just go do it," Joe said, "I'll teach you what I know but nobody knows it all when it comes to wild turkeys. They're still kind of a mystery. They sometimes do things that you can't explain. As you hunt 'em more and more, you'll see some of that for yourself."

When they arrived at the Johnson house they climbed the steps and knocked on the front door. Mrs. Johnson opened the screen door, "Hello, Joe. Hey, Connor. Good to see y'all."

"Hello, Velma," Joe said, "I picked a few more turnips today and I can't eat them all so I hope you can use them."

"Oh, yes, sir, thank you so much," she said. "Connor, the boys went over to Mr. Owens place to cut the grass. Those boys mow his grass every summer. He just ain't able to do it anymore and Kenny likes to earn money any chance he gets. They'll be back late this afternoon. Janice is here working on her sewing. That girl loves to sew. Y'all come on in and set a spell."

"Well, thank you, Velma," Joe said, "but I got some more work to do back home."

Connor stood on the porch holding his baseball glove.

Mrs. Johnson noticed it. "Connor, why don't you stay here for a while. The boys should be back later. Aubrey can give you a ride back home."

Connor went inside.

Janice came out of a back room, "Hey there."

"Hey there," Connor said. "So, you can sew? Ha, that sounded funny."

"Yeah, I like to sew. Come see what I'm working on."

81

Connor followed Janice to the back room where an electric sewing machine sat against the wall with a large piece of yellow fabric draped across the machine.

"This is my Easter dress. I hope I can finish it in time."

"It's a pretty color. Did you make that dress you had on Sunday?"

"Yeah, you liked it?"

"Yeah, it looked really good," he said with a little too much enthusiasm. "I mean … it looked like … you know … store-bought."

Janice grinned, "You're shy, ain't ya?"

Connor didn't respond. He stared at the floor.

"I like that. It's better than being, you know … loud," she giggled.

"I guess so," he said, smiling.

They spent the afternoon together. They tossed Kenny's baseball back and forth, then sat in the swing, each with a glass of sweet tea Mrs. Johnson had handed them.

Connor found it easy to talk to Janice.

~~~~~~

Later, as Mr. Johnson drove Connor back home, he studied Connor. His voice became quiet and sincere, "We all think the world of Mr. Joe. Everybody does. He's a good neighbor and you are lucky to have him as your grandpa, son."

"Yes, sir. I know that for sure. He's teaching me a lot about hunting and taking care of the chickens … and the garden, too."

"Yep, Mr. Joe has always liked them animals and birds. He probably knows more about turkeys than anybody around. We sho' was sad when your grandma passed; she was a fine lady."

"When is Janice's birthday, Mr. Johnson?" Connor blurted out. He had totally forgotten to pose the question to Janice.

"April twelfth. She's gonna be fourteen. My goodness, them kids are growin' up quick."

"Yes, sir," Connor said as his mind started twirling.

I could get her a gift. I wonder if there would be a party?

When they arrived, Connor thanked Mr. Johnson for the ride home, got out of the truck, ran up the front steps, and through the front door. "Hey, Paw Paw, I'm home."

He thought about what he'd said. *Home.* He considered it for a few seconds then figured … it was okay with him.

Joe came through the back door, "Okay, son, we've had our fun for the day. Now it's time to put in some work."

Connor assisted his grandfather repairing the hole under the chicken pen.

During the afternoon, they drove south along Rocky Hill Road to a place where a patch of tall canes grew. They sawed a pile of cane and hauled it home to use for tomato stakes.

After supper, they watched the local news on television while planning to go after the "durn ole' turkey" that had hung-up Sunday morning at Jones Bluff.

During a lull in the conversation, Connor said, "Paw Paw, what you said about all boys feeling the way I do … what about girls?"

With a wide grin, Joe said, "I wouldn't know about girls, son, I've never been one. Besides, if you can figure them out, you'd be the first one to do it."

Connor rubbed his hands down his pants leg, "How do you make a girl like you, Paw Paw?"

"You can't *make* them like you. All you can do is be yourself and hope they like you for who you are. But, what a girl wants more than anything is to be heard. They like to know somebody will listen. I figured that much out about them a long time ago."

Connor leaned back in his chair, put his hands behind his neck, staring at the ceiling, "I think Janice likes me."

"I'm pretty sure you're right. Now, just be yourself and always show her respect, then y'all might stay friends a long time."

Connor turned his eyes toward his grandfather, "I like our talks, Paw Paw."

"Me too, son. Now, let's hit the sack so we can be at our best for ole Mr. Turkey in the morning. Okay?"

"Yes, sir."

~~~~~~

Before sleep came, Joe considered their conversations. These talks let him understand Connor better while learning what Connor worried about. Connor seemed happier than when he'd first arrived. His features were less tense, his jittery posture had relaxed and his demeanor seemed calmer.

Having family here had also revealed how lonesome Joe had been. Joe relaxed while anticipating what the future held for his grandson. Peaceful sleep came over him.

CHAPTER 16 – ACROSS THE CREEK

Mosquitoes swarmed as Joe and Connor arrived at Jones Bluff on Wednesday morning. The air was heavy and humid, with the temperature more like summer than spring. Joe rubbed his hands with repellent, applying it to his face and neck. He sprayed his shirtsleeves, then his pants, before handing the spray to Connor. Connor copied the process.

Joe withdrew two pieces of army-green cloth, handing one to Connor.

"When we get set up, wrap this around your face from your nose down and tie it off. It will help keep the mosquitoes from biting. We'll spray the cloth before we tie it on."

Connor stuffed the cloth in his pocket as they made their way to the crest of the hill. Joe owled at daylight but got no response. After fifteen minutes of owling, daylight was upon them. Joe placed the diaphragm call in his mouth to make several loud cuts and yelps.

"I heard one," Connor whispered.

Joe wrinkled his nose, "You did? I didn't hear him. Where's he at?"

"Way off down that way." Connor pointed to the east. "I could barely hear him."

"Let's go. Maybe my old ears can hear him from down there."

They hiked two hundred yards to the east until they reached the edge of a wide creek, stopping for Joe to call again.

The tom answered from across the creek. He sounded so far, Joe thought there was little hope of getting the turkey to come, especially across the wide creek.

But he did answer the call, so why not see what happens? There's nothing to lose.

For the next thirty minutes, Joe called. The turkey answered occasionally. They couldn't tell if it moved closer or remained in the same spot from so far away. Joe handed the call to Connor. "Give him a try," he said.

Connor had practiced with the box call every chance he got back at the house. Joe critiqued his calling whenever he heard Connor practice. Connor could make several calls adequately, including the yelp, cluck, purr and cut.

He hesitated but took the call from Joe, making a series of loud yelps. When the tom answered, Connor's eyes widened as he smiled at Joe. He repeated the call several times until eventually the turkey stopped responding.

Joe figured the gobbler had finally attracted a hen, then shut up. Nevertheless, they waited for another thirty minutes in case the tom moved their way. Joe figured if the tom was coming he would gobble when he got close, trying to locate the hen that had been mouthing off all morning.

"Sometimes, they'll just fly across the creek toward you when they answer from far away," Joe explained, "He may come to this area, then gobble. He knows exactly where your calling came from, even from far away, but sometimes he'll announce himself when he's in the area to try to make the hen let him know where she's at. So, we need to sit here a while and wait, just in case."

After another ten minutes without hearing a turkey sound, Joe crow-called several times, trying to make the tom gobble. No response came, so Joe decided to give up, heading for an early breakfast at the café.

"You can never expect to see a turkey every time you go. If you hear one, then you're doing good," Joe reminded Connor on the way to the café. "We know he's there. It's just a matter of time before we can see him."

"Seems like you never get disappointed, Paw Paw."

Joe chuckled, "Not with turkey hunting, I don't. If I did that, I would have gave up a long time ago."

They ordered their food, discussing today's hunt. Jessie Pickens came through the door. He sat with them, ordering coffee. Jessie was passing through Uriah, heading to the office from a logging site where problems occurred with a truck. The job site sat across the highway from the state prison.

The old friends talked for thirty minutes over several cups of coffee.

Jessie took an interest in Connor, too. During the conversation, he joked, "Now, if your Paw Paw ever runs out of work for you, I can always use a saw-hand on the logging crew."

After a chuckle, Joe said, "I heard Mrs. Baker wants to retire."

"Yeah, I can't talk her out of it. Gonna be a lot different around there without her," Jessie said.

After they left the café, Connor questioned Joe about the logging business.

"It takes a strong man to handle those saws all day long," Joe said. "You've got some growing to do if you want to be a logger. But, I don't recommend that kind of work. No sir, not at all. It's dirty and dangerous. It will wear a man down before his time. I was lucky to get a job at the power company whenever I was young. It was good steady work and the retirement pay is fine, too. Me and your Maw Maw did okay."

CHAPTER 17 - CRAWDADS

When Joe turned off the bumpy county road onto Rocky Hill Road heading home, they noticed it had been graded. The smooth surface left by the big machine made for a smooth ride. When they neared their driveway, Connor noticed bicycle tracks in the fresh-graded red dirt. In addition, he noticed footprints there, too. He quickly determined he had missed a visit from the Johnson kids.

"Paw Paw, I wanna' go down to the creek to see if they are still down there, okay?" Connor said.

"Sure. If you get hungry, just come home and we'll eat. If not, be home before dark. I guess you deserve a day without chores. After all, it *is* your vacation week."

After they parked, Connor quickly vaulted out, jogging the road toward the spot where it bridged the little creek, a half mile away. He read footprints in the fresh dirt, recognizing two different size shoe prints, along with the lines from the bicycle tires.

As he approached the creek, voices signaled the Johnson kids location. He spotted the old rusty bicycle first, leaning against a tree off the road, down a well-worn trail following along the edge of the creek. Lying in the trail, beside the bike, he noticed two pair of worn shoes.

The trail, crooked and muddy in spots, with roots from nearby trees protruding from the ground, made the walk difficult. He followed the trail into the woods, along the creek bank. Once the road fell twenty yards behind him, the surrounding woods became more open. The sunlight from the open road provided the plants there what they needed to grow tall and thick. Once the ground became shaded, the plants grew low under the canopy of tall trees in the creek bottom.

He spotted Kenny first, calf-deep in the cold stream, bent over at the waist, talking to his brother. "Don't move so quick, Clay, you'll scare everything off," he said.

"I ain't," Clay replied.

"Hey, y'all," Connor said.

They glanced around.

Connor saw Janice raise her head from the other side of a tree trunk, which had fallen across the creek. The leaves on the tree were budding even in its horizontal position. She smiled, waving as she stepped out of the creek, up the bank to the trail. She wore jeans, rolled up above her knees, with a pink tee shirt.

"Hey, Connor," she said, "We came by your house to see if you were home but your granddaddy's truck was gone."

"Yeah, I saw your tracks and followed them down here," Connor said with a proud smile.

"You're a regular Daniel Boone," she teased.

Kenny invited Connor to get in the creek, offering to show him how to catch crawdads. He noticed Clay, the younger brother, had a small net. Janice held a cotton string with a raw chicken neck tied to the end. Kenny did also.

Clay still had his tennis shoes on moving slowly upstream, searching the shallow water.

"Just ease along and watch for 'em," Kenny said. "They're hard to see until you get good at it. Sometimes, if you see a big rock you can ease it toward you and see them move away from it. If you pull the rock too quick, it'll muddy the water then you won't see nothin'. If you see one, you can catch him with your hand or you can put the chicken neck in front of him and he'll hang on to the meat all the way to the top of the water, when you pull it up. Then it's easy to grab 'em. We let Clay use the net since he's the youngest. Besides, we can catch 'em a lot better than he can."

"I can catch 'em as good as you!" Clay yelled in protest.

For the next thirty minutes, Connor tried his best to locate a crawdad. Everyone else caught them often. The Johnsons dropped their catch into a five-gallon bucket partly filled with creek water.

Connor glanced at Janice, "What do y'all do with these crawdads?"

"Kenny sells them to Mr. Hudson. He runs catfish lines for a living down at the river. He uses them for bait when he can get them. He says they're the best bait in the world."

"How much do y'all get for a bucket full?"

"Sometimes as much as five dollars. It just depends if Mr. Hudson has been drinking or not. When he's drinking, he pays *good*." She giggled.

"I just can't see 'em," Connor complained.

"They look like a black rock on the bottom. They swim backwards but they can move quick if they're scared."

Connor spotted something between two rocks. The crawdad's camouflage failed when it moved its claws. Connor snatched it from the water. The crustacean stretched three inches long. He held it out toward Janice, "Look, I got … ouch!" Connor dropped the crawfish back in the water, shaking his hand, then sticking his finger in his mouth, "He bit me."

The Johnson kids howled with laughter. After they caught their breath, Kenny said, "Man, you gotta hold them bigguns right behind their head so they can't pinch you."

Connor laughed with them. He continued to search for more crawdads, determined to get one in the bucket. By the end of the first hour, Connor became a more proficient crawdad catcher. Janice moved up the narrow creek close beside him, often holding on to his shoulder to balance. His senses heightened each time she did it.

Whenever Janice caught a crawdad, Connor grabbed the bucket to hold it close, letting her drop her catch inside. She always smiled, gazing directly into his face to say "Thank you," with a sweet tone.

Connor lost track of time. His mind distracted, catching crawdads became secondary.

Flirting is fun.

When the bucket became half-full of bubbling, squirming crawfish, Kenny announced they'd caught enough, then ambled to the road to carry the heavy bucket home. He invited Connor to come along.

"We'll take these to Mr. Hudson later when Daddy goes that way again," Janice said. "He lives way down at the river, up the hill from the landing. He's usually always home in the afternoon when he finishes running his lines."

"How do you keep them alive?"

"We fill the bucket all the way up with water and cover the top with a piece of lumber. Sometimes, we have to keep the water changed out if we keep them for more than a day or two. As long as they're kept cool, they do all right," she said.

Connor focused … with a new idea, "Hey, if I get Paw Paw to take us fishing, do you think you could go?"

"Well, maybe so. I'll ask Daddy tonight and let you know."

"I hope you can. It'll be fun. I love to fish, don't you?"

"Yeah, but I never catch anything. Do y'all go in a boat?"

"Yep, Paw Paw has a little boat. He likes to catch white perch."

"I've never been fishing in a boat."

"It's so much fun. I hope you get to go."

"Me too." Janice cocked her head to one side, raising one eyebrow. "Do you have a girlfriend in Mobile?"

The question surprised Connor. He stopped, contemplating her for a moment with wide eyes. "No, I never, I mean … uh, no I don't."

Connor thought of something to add. It came to him out of nowhere, pleasing him that he'd thought of something so clever. He twisted one side of his mouth into a wry smile. "But I'd like to have one in Uriah."

She shifted to see his smile, then returned one to him. "I think that could happen," she winked, blushing.

Connor would never again be the same.

Afterward, Connor realized he had no idea if his grandfather would take them fishing or even if the boat motor still worked. It had been over a year since the last time they used it together.

~~~~~~~

"Mama, Janice has a boyfriend!" Clay yelled as he ran through the front door of his house. He'd run far ahead of the others once they got to the edge of the yard. Clay, at eleven years old, had realized there was *"something up"* with his sister and this new boy. He couldn't wait to let his mother in on the big news he'd discovered.

In the kitchen, Mrs. Velma Johnson flipped the dishtowel over her shoulder when she heard him. She met him at the kitchen entrance, then bent over, taking his shoulders in her hands. She moved her face close to his, whispering, "Now you listen, Clay, that's not nice to say it the way you did. We will talk about this later when your daddy's home. I don't want to hear another word about this until then, you hear?"

Clay stared wide-eyed at his mama. "Yes, ma'am," he said, his face downcast. Clay didn't quite understand but he knew when his mother had laid down the law.

The set of Mrs. Johnson's jaw conveyed her determination. She'd not let her only daughter be subjected to the same ridicule she had endured as a teen. She'd had six brothers and three sisters. They had teased her constantly the first time she showed interest in a boy. It got so bad, she never got over it completely. She promised herself to make sure, if Janice liked a boy, she wouldn't be teased. She would make sure the boy came from a good upbringing, first. He must treat her daughter with respect. She'd demand the same respect from Janice's brothers—no teasing allowed. It was time to have a talk about it.

Tonight, there's going to be a family meeting.

Connor, Kenny and Janice were too far behind Clay to hear when he yelled the news to his mama. Velma Johnson gave thanks that Clay's comment had not embarrassed her daughter.

~~~~~~

The four youngsters ate a peanut butter sandwich lunch. After lunch, Kenny filled the crawdad bucket with water from the outside water spigot. They sat on the porch for a time talking, then played some catch.

Connor plodded home under the cool afternoon shade of trees along the freshly graded road. On the way, he rehearsed what he would say to his Paw Paw when he approached the subject of the fishing trip.

When he passed the little creek where they had caught crawdads earlier, a deer stepped into the road fifty yards ahead. The deer stopped in the road, raised its head, gazing along the road at Connor. On top of the deer's head, Connor saw two dark circles where the buck had shed its antlers. Connor froze. He'd never seen a bigger deer. The buck gazed at Connor,

93

flipped its tail once, then lowering its head, continued calmly to the other side of the road. It melted into the tall pines. When Connor scampered to where the deer had passed, he found large deep tracks in the loose red dirt.

Connor raised both hands high in the air, leaned back, yelling toward the sky. "Woo Hoo!" He could hardly wait to tell Joe about the close encounter with a big buck.

CHAPTER 18 – SNAKE SKIN

The Johnson household became busy that night. Mr. Johnson had spent the day repairing lawn mower engines for two different families at their respective homes. Business was good when grass began growing again each spring. He arrived home at six o'clock.

As soon as he received the customary welcome-home kiss from his wife, she said, "We're having a meeting with the kids tonight."

"Okay," he said flatly. After twenty-five years of marriage to Velma, curiosity was not as powerful as it once was. He knew the subject of the meeting would be revealed to him in good time.

"I want to make sure everybody understands that Janice is growing up now and that if she likes Connor, it's okay. He seems like a nice boy and I don't want her to feel like there's anything wrong with liking a boy or having a special friend."

"Okay," Aubrey replied with the same matter of fact tone as before. Then in a lighter tone said, "So ... what's for supper?"

"Aubrey Johnson, I swear," she said, playfully swatting his face with the dishtowel from her shoulder.

After supper, they gathered in the living room where Mrs. Johnson made her case to the family. She explained, in her gentle way, that the changes in Janice's feelings are part of the natural world.

"It's as natural as an ole snake that sheds its old skin and grows a new one."

Velma Johnson continued, explaining how they were all to be extra careful about what they said to each other.

She told Janice, "You are not to be ashamed or shy about how your feelings may be changing."

She focused special attention on Clay during the family talk.

She noticed how Clay sat tight to the back of his chair, wrapping his arms around his knees, as if feeling her eyes burning the words into his brain.

Velma realized Kenny did not need to listen closely to her lecture. He was already old enough to understand everything she was trying to say.

~~~~~

Kenny knew that his mother's instructions were mainly for the benefit of his siblings. He liked Connor, long since accepting the fact his sister would be hounded by awkward, young boys. Kenny would watch out for his sister, as his daddy had instructed, and keep a keen eye out for any boys being disrespectful.

~~~~~

Janice sat quietly, soaking it in. She loved how her mama protected her, wanting her to be happy, although she was still a little embarrassed. She was glad that her younger brother was being warned. He could be *such a pain*, but she knew he meant no harm.

I do not like being compared to a snake. Eww.

She noticed how her father treated her mother. She watched him as he listened attentively, nodding his head in agreement with many of his wife's instructions, while occasionally flashing a glance at Clay to let him know that he'd be much better off if he took his mama's instructions seriously.

Janice decided she should wait until tomorrow to ask if she could go fishing. Tonight, she thought, it would be too much, too soon.

That night, as the whip-o-wills called outside her window, Janice Johnson, almost fourteen years old, hugged her feather pillow, feeling a little closer to becoming a woman.

~~~~~~

During supper, Connor said, "Paw Paw, do you think we could go fishing later this week in the boat?"

"Maybe so," Joe replied. "I think the water's come back down from the flood we had earlier. Should be able to catch a few around the cypress knees. The perch might be spawning about now."

"Great. Can I invite somebody?"

"I suppose so, son. Just who did you have in mind?" He gave Connor a deadpan stare. "Your new buddy Kenny?" Then the corner of his mouth rose slightly.

Connor knew his grandfather teased him but it contained no malice.

"No, sir."

Joe chuckled. "If it's okay with her parents, it's okay with me."

Nancy called at seven PM.

Connor answered on the first ring.

She inquired about his day, asking about the hunt that morning.

Connor missed his mother but didn't let on much. Finally, he got around to the important question.

"Mom, Janice's birthday is April twelfth and I want to buy her something. I still have the ten dollars you gave me. I'm clueless as to what I can get her."

"Well, does she wear any jewelry?"

"I don't know. I mean, I didn't notice."

"Most girls that age like jewelry. Why don't I pick out something this week, and I'll bring it this weekend? If you like it, we can wrap it later."

"You think that's what she wants?"

"I'm not sure what she wants, but I'm sure she'll appreciate the thought. I'll buy something I think she will like. Just leave it to me."

"Okay, Mom. I'll pay you back when you get here."

"Yes, you will. And, *you're welcome, Connor.*"

"Thanks, Mama."

After the busy day, Connor went to bed early. He dropped into a deep sleep, dreaming he steered a big blue boat along a river. The choppy water teemed with crawdads splashing all around the boat. A turkey gobbled. When he twisted to see, the tom was roosted on the tip of the bow. Janice was sitting beside the turkey gobbler with her feet hanging over the side of the boat. She gazed at him saying, "Come on in," as she lowered herself into the water. Connor jerked awake in a cold sweat. His throat ached, stinging when he swallowed. His head was heavy as if full of water.

The next morning he staggered into the kitchen. Joe straightened from the oven where he heated their sausage biscuits. He bent over to pour food into Belle's dish. Surveying Connor he asked, "You okay? You look a little tired this morning."

"Yes, sir, I'm okay," Connor's voice was an octave lower than usual.

"I don't think so, son. You sound like you're getting a cold to me."

"Yes, sir. I think I'll be okay. I still want to go hunting. Maybe just a little while, anyways."

Joe laid the back of his hand on Connor's forehead. "Well, no fever that I can tell. We'll just go back to Jones Bluff this morning. It'll be a short hunt. Here, take these," Joe handed Connor two aspirins.

Joe figured the best medicine for a spring cold was fresh morning air with a little exercise. It often worked for Joe, loosening up a clogged head. If the boy felt bad later in the morning, he'd make him stay inside today to rest. *Maybe some chicken soup later.*

After they hiked to the listening spot at Jones Bluff, Connor reported he felt better but not normal. The gobbler did not make a sound that morning. In fact, they heard no turkey sounds at all.

Joe decided they'd sit, then "blind-call" occasionally. He explained that blind-calling is something you can do when the toms won't gobble. "You sit still and call every fifteen or twenty minutes hoping one comes to you. You have to stay still and quiet because you never know when one will show up. It works sometimes but it's not the most fun. The excitement comes from calling one to you, hearing him respond and tricking the ole boy to come close."

They sat for another hour. Nothing showed up. When they got up to leave the setup, they heard a turkey fly out of a tree about seventy-five yards in front of them.

After the turkey flew away, Joe said, "That turkey sat there the whole morning, Connor. He probably heard us or caught a glimpse of us but wasn't sure what to do until we got up to leave."

Connor was amazed at these turkeys. How wily and unpredictable they were. The more he learned about them, the more he respected them. It made him even more proud of the one he'd killed already.

Back at home, Joe took some chicken from the freezer to begin making soup. "You rest today, buddy. After lunch, you can watch the TV, and this afternoon I need to go to the feed store. Tomorrow, I want to plant beans."

Connor found the homemade chicken soup delicious. He ate two bowls for lunch then fell asleep on the couch for two hours. When he awoke, the scratchy throat and stuffy head had gone.

Chicken soup is amazing.

They rode together to the feed store at three-thirty. Joe bought a pound of snap bean seeds plus several bags of triple-eight fertilizer. He also bought two sacks of cracked corn for the chickens. Connor loaded the fertilizer with the feed corn in the truck bed.

They stopped at the gas station to fill the truck. Joe commented on how the price had gone up a penny per gallon. It had risen to thirty-three cents.

While at the station, Joe also filled a red metal can with gasoline for the boat. When they got home, Joe connected the gas tank to the boat motor then attached a water hose to the bottom of the engine near the propeller before he cranked the engine.

"It's louder than I remember," Connor said, covering his ears.

"That's because it's out of the water."

Joe allowed it to idle for five minutes. "Seems to have survived the winter just fine." Joe killed the engine. "She's ready to go fishing."

CHAPTER 19 – CLEAR VIEW

Connor woke before Joe the next morning, using the time to beat Joe into the kitchen. He snatched two biscuits from the refrigerator, wrapped them in tinfoil before putting them in the oven he'd set to three-hundred-fifty degrees. He didn't know how to make coffee, so he didn't try. He made a mental note to ask for instructions later.

When Joe came into the kitchen, he asked, "How you feeling this morning?"

"I'm better, Paw Paw. Are we going back to Jones Bluff again?"

"No, I think we'll try the Hall Place today. It's been a week since I killed a turkey there. I think there were two more longbeards in the area. The birds ought to be settled down now, letting the pecking order get back to normal. We should be able to hear one over there today."

"Can I call again today, Paw Paw?"

"I tell you what, why don't you do everything today? I'll just sit back and watch the show."

"Well, okay. But you'll let me know if I mess up?"

Joe chuckled, "I don't think I'll *need* to tell you but, yeah, if you mess up, I'll tell you."

Joe led Connor to the same tree where he'd sat on opening morning. "This here's my favorite place to sit. I opened most of the last twenty seasons in this spot."

As more light came into the sky, Connor could see the area better and understood why Paw Paw considered the place special. It reminded Connor of a book he'd seen with a painting of an enchanted forest.

They sat in silence as the first light of day brightened the woods. They listened for the birds to wake. A distant owl laughed. The sound of an owl "laughing," as Paw Paw called it, was an eerie sound, reminding Connor of the sound of excited chimpanzees he'd seen on Tarzan movies.

Dawn broke. The birds became active, flitting around the area. Connor cradled the box call in both hands. With his right hand, he pinched the end of the lid between his fingers, applying pressure to the edge of the box while moving the lid quickly across, reducing the pressure as it moved. It produced a deep cluck. He repeated the process seconds later. Connor placed the call on the ground, returning his hands to the gunstock.

A minute or two passed before the tom gobbled. Connor couldn't tell if the tom had answered his call or if the tom had gobbled on his own. He waited. The turkey eventually gobbled again.

Connor picked up the call carefully to send two more distinctive clucks. The bird gobbled during Connor's second cluck, cutting off his call.

Connor was unsure what to do now. He wanted to whisper to his grandfather for advice.

Should I yelp now or should I shut up and wait?

Connor reconsidered; he decided to stay quiet for a while. He'd be better off being more safe than sorry.

The turkey gobbled several more times from his roost. He was located at least one hundred fifty yards in the swamp bottom; slightly to the right of the direction Connor and Joe were faced. They waited, listening for the sound of the gobbler flying down from his roost. They listened for hens. They heard a distant crow, which encouraged the turkey to gobble again.

At seventy-five yards, slightly to their left, Connor caught movement. He strained his eyes to focus on what he saw. Something slinked along the edge of the swamp in a steady, slow pace. A bobcat materialized in the swamp's brushy border. The cat glided along, stalking across Connor's left to his right. He slipped between the hunters and the swamp, never knowing they hid nearby. Connor didn't know if this was good or bad or if it would affect the turkey hunt. He wasn't sure if he should do anything, so he sat still, watching the cat saunter by.

After the cat slid from sight, Connor leaned his head to glance at his grandfather. His grandfather did not say anything. He remained motionless with the green cloth tied around his face; only his eyes visible. Connor could not read anything in Joe's eyes.

When Connor slowly rotated his neck to face forward, the turkey gobbled again. The gobble had a different tone.

The turkey's on the ground.

Connor knew the tom was still in the swamp but coming closer. He could hardly believe his luck.

Is he coming to my call? Should I call again and, if so, what call should I use?

Connor's panic rose inside him. He questioned his decision to remain silent as his heart raced.

Connor decided to put his cheek against the stock, keeping both eyes open while waiting for the turkey to show up. Silent minutes passed.

Then everything happened at once. The tom was there, directly to the front of him, his head held high.

How did he come out of nowhere like that?

The turkey strutted into a clear, open lane in front, straight down the gun barrel.

103

Connor aimed, pulling the trigger. The tom hopped, spreading his wings wide. He was airborne toward the swamp in no time, his wings beating against small limbs in the trees on his way.

Connor's stomach lurched. His hands and arms shook while his eyes watered. He puckered his lips, spitting a foul sound then stomped his foot against the ground.

Connor spun to his Paw Paw, wide-eyed in bewilderment, "What happened?"

Joe pulled the cloth from his face, smiling at Connor. "You missed."

"I had the bead right on his neck, Paw Paw," Connor pleaded.

"Yep, I think you did, but that turkey was over fifty yards away."

As if a gong sounded, Connor realized what the old man said. He studied where the bird had been. In the clear, open woods, the big turkey looked close enough to shoot. Connor had done everything right, up until the last two seconds of the hunt. He'd become too anxious and not let the tom come closer, into gun range.

"It's hard not to shoot when he's in the wide open, ain't it?" Joe said smiling.

"Yes, sir. I guess so," Connor said in a quiet voice.

Before going home, they scouted along the power line, then a nearby field, scanning for strut marks and dusting. They discovered some hen tracks in dusting areas. Small indentions made in the dry, sandy dirt, each the size of a dinner plate where turkeys had wallowed, kicking dirt up into their feathers.

Joe said, "They dust themselves to get rid of mites. It's their way of taking a bath."

Connor dropped his chin to his chest, "Yes, sir," still struggling to accept he'd missed. Especially when he'd called his first one on his own.

"You're not the only one to ever miss a turkey, son. But you should be proud that you called him to you. Not many boys your age have done it."

Connor understood the purpose of his grandpa's comments. They were meant to ease his disappointment. He appreciated the effort but it didn't help.

Connor wished he had waited. He longed to blame something other than his own impatience. More than anything else, he chomped at the bit for another chance.

CHAPTER 20 - TIMBER

During lunch, Joe received a call from Jessie Pickens. "Joe, there's a timber buyer from Scott Paper in Monroeville for a few days. I just found out he likes to turkey hunt. I wanted to ask you before I offered him a hunt."

"That's fine with me, Jessie. Maybe he can hunt Saturday morning, and then we could meet him, too. I planned on taking Connor up there. I'd like to meet another turkey hunter. They're kinda few and far between."

"I'll ask him. I'll see y'all Saturday then."

Joe told Connor the news. Connor was anxious to meet another man who hunted turkey.

~~~~~~

Janice approached her father who worked on a mower in the back yard. Someone had brought it for repair. She spoke softly, "Daddy, would you mind if I went fishing in a boat with Mr. Parker and Connor sometime?"

Aubrey Johnson stopped twisting the wrench he used before facing his daughter. "When?"

"I don't know yet, Daddy. I wanted to talk to you first."

He studied her face for a moment, then focused again on the wrench, "Go ask your mama. If it's okay with her, I guess it'll be alright."

Janice ran toward the house. She already knew her mother would say yes once she told her Daddy had said yes.

~~~~~~~

Connor and Joe spent the afternoon in the garden. They opened seven straight rows in the dirt with the edge of their hoes. They spread fertilizer into the rows, then chopped each row with hoes, mixing the fertilizer into the grey dirt. They dropped the seeds into each open row as they plodded along the side of each one. In the last step, using the hoes, they covered the seeds with soil about an inch deep.

When they finished planting the beans, they spent the latter part of the day cleaning the chicken pen. They shoveled the chicken manure from the ground, placing it in buckets. The buckets were then emptied by spreading the contents under pear, peach and pecan trees around the property.

"Chicken manure is a strong fertilizer. Don't put out too much on any one tree, it'll burn the roots," Joe warned.

Connor admired the woods around the farm as he worked, "Paw Paw, you ever heard a turkey gobble around here?"

"Nope, in all my years here, there's never been any turkeys close by. Maybe one day they'll be here," Joe said. "I'd like to be able to sit on the porch and just listen to one someday."

Connor collapsed, tired and dirty, when evening came. After a bath, they ate supper, washed the dishes, and sat in the living room. Joe rubbed Belle's ears as she sat between his knees.

"Connor, you know, your Maw Maw never allowed a dog in the house. After she passed, I had no reason to leave Belle outside at night anymore. She does fine inside, she won't chew on anything unless I give it to her. I think she likes having you here."

"Does she still fetch birds in the dove fields?"

"Oh sure, she still loves it." Joe chuckled. "And, she'll tree squirrels but she can't follow them if they timber. She never has caught on to that."

"What does 'timber' mean?"

"That's when a squirrel jumps from one tree to another."

"Paw Paw, how long will she live?"

"Don't know. I think she has a few more good years."

Connor thought about his father. After six months, he still didn't understand. He pondered how different things would be if he still lived. He wondered if he'd be here during Spring Break with his grandpa.

He considered Paw Paw's age. He forced the thought from his mind, kneeling on the floor to play with Belle, a happy distraction.

Later, as Connor lay in bed, he buried his head in his pillow and fought the tears.

CHAPTER 21 – WINDBURN

The turkeys did not gobble. Day broke windy, with high clouds rolling across the morning sky. Jones Bluff seemed desolate. To Connor, it became depressing. Nothing like a few days before.

After an hour of loud crow calling and scouting, Joe said, "It's not a good day to hear a turkey. The wind cuts down the distance we can hear them. It limits how far they can hear our calls. Turkeys will stay in the fields most of the day today. Even if you find them there, it's hard to call them out of a field on a windy day. Let's go to the café, then we'll plan the rest of the day."

"Yes, sir," Connor said. "Maybe we can take a closer look at the school while we're up in town."

Joe thought about what the boy said.

Up in town. Hmm, there ain't much of a town to be up in.

One filling station, a grocery, two cafés, one hardware store, the cotton gin north on Hwy 21. The intersection where Hwy 59 merged into Hwy 21 formed the only significant intersection; it consisted of one stop sign. On the other hand, the town had two big churches. The Baptist and the Methodist. That's it. Joe liked it that way.

Most employed folks living in or around the community worked in the timber industry. Some were loggers. Some worked at a sawmill twenty-five miles north. A few had a job at the prison, six miles east. Some men traveled all the way to Mobile for work. The remainder farmed.

They arrived at the café at seven-thirty. Glen Pace was the only customer. When they came through the door, Glen said, "Don't tell me you done killed another turkey, Joe."

"Naw, Glen, we didn't even hear one this morning," Joe said. "You remember my grandson, Connor?" Joe gestured toward the boy. "This is Mr. Pace, son," the man shook Connor's hand.

"Connor's going to school here Monday," Joe told Glen.

They talked over coffee and eggs. Glen told Connor that four of his grandsons went to the local high school. "I'll make sure they all introduce theyselves to you at school Monday."

"I'm looking forward to going here. I want to try out for the baseball team. I've already made a few friends here," Connor said.

"I think you'll like the coach. He teaches Sunday school at the Methodist Church. He's a good feller," Glen said. "They had a good team last year. I hope they're good this year, too, although they lost a few seniors along with a great pitcher."

Joe had told Connor earlier that any of the school games drew big crowds. Baseball, basketball, and football games served as the only entertainment folks had here, besides church activities. It didn't surprise Connor that Mr. Pace was a fan.

After breakfast, they rode by the empty school as Connor studied the layout. Joe said he wanted to take a trip to the river to see how the water was clearing. Heavy spring rains farther north in central Alabama caused the river here to rise out of its banks, staying high for more than a week in February.

"I'm thinking if we make sure to get back from Beatrice early tomorrow, we can get in some fishing in the afternoon. I doubt Mrs. Johnson is going to let Janice go fishing on a Sunday," Joe said.

Connor hadn't thought of that. Fishing on Sunday was considered a sin. Tomorrow would be the last day for fishing before school began again on Monday. He had to get in touch with Janice today to see if she'd gotten permission. If she did, he would ask her to go tomorrow.

"Do you have the Johnson's phone number, Paw Paw?"

"They don't have a phone. But, if you want to go see them, I can take you by there."

"Okay. That'll do."

Connor had already begun to use some of the same phrases he'd heard from Joe.

They drove past home on the way to the Johnson's. Connor peered through the trees into the front yard as they passed. He could see Belle run from the porch to greet them. Connor knew Belle recognized the sound of Joe's truck coming down Rocky Hill Road, fully expecting the truck to swerve into the driveway. As Connor peered through the rear window, he could see Belle stop and sit, watching in bewilderment as the truck continued down the road. Connor's stomach curled in a knot. He didn't understand how seeing Belle's disappointment made his eyes water. Connor, thinking about his father, stared out the passenger window until they arrived.

When they pulled into the Johnson's yard, Janice sat on the front porch swing. Mr. Johnson worked under the hood of his old truck. Joe strolled to the truck, visiting with Mr. Johnson, while Connor jogged to the front porch.

Later, when they returned to the truck, Connor said Janice had received permission to go. "We can pick her up tomorrow afternoon."

Joe already knew all of this from his conversation with Aubrey Johnson, but didn't let on.

"I think we could do some tractor work today," Joe said. "We'll hook up the bush-hog and mow the field. Those weeds are getting pretty tall. I'll be wanting to plow before long. If I let them weeds get too tall, they clog up my plow."

"Can I drive the tractor today?"

"Yep, I reckon so if you'll go slow and be careful."

~~~~~

Connor worked the rest of the day mowing the field on the tractor. Joe insisted he run in first gear, which made the going slow. Connor loved being in control of the powerful machine. He counted the field rats hopping across the grass, escaping the oncoming, noisy intruder. The rats hopped like rabbits. Occasionally, Belle would see one, catching it before it could get away. *There is so much fun to be had in the country,* he thought as he eased along on the tractor. *I'm never going to leave this place again.*

That night his head and face grew hot from windburn. He splashed his face with cold water, wrapped a few pieces of ice in a dishtowel, holding it against his face after supper.

Tomorrow would be a big day. He expected to meet the new turkey-hunting man. Later in the day, he planned to take Janice on her first fishing trip in a boat. Connor went to bed early so tomorrow would come quicker.

CHAPTER 22 – MR. KELLY

Connor's eyes popped open as the alarm clattered at three AM. He pulled the curtain from the window to survey the sky. Stars blanketed the black sky so he knew the weather was clear; a good sign.

Paw Paw says turkeys gobble better in clear weather.

The drive to Beatrice seemed to take longer than the last time, but they arrived at five thirty, noticing there were two trucks parked in front of Jessie Pickens's house. They recognized Jessie's truck. Connor figured the other truck belonged to Jessie's guest. The logo on the truck's door, barely visible, since the truck carried a film of red mud, read *Scott Paper*.

They could hear voices inside the house when they stepped on the porch. Through the screen door they saw Jessie standing in the kitchen with a coffee pot in his hand. Another man sat at the kitchen table.

Joe pulled the screen door, letting himself in. Connor followed.

"Come on in, y'all," Jessie said. "Joe, this here is Mr. Tom Kelly. Tom, this is Joe Parker and that's his grandson, Connor."

They sat at the table after handshakes went around. Jessie poured them each a cup of hot coffee. Connor spooned some sugar from the bowl on the table, adding it to his cup while the conversations got going.

113

Tom Kelly had a distinctive voice. His tone was deep and steady with a little gravel added for flavor. His friendly eyes seemed to sparkle as he turned his attention to Connor. "Young man, Jessie tells me you and your grandpa are afflicted with the same sad disease that I have. Not everybody can be a turkey hunter. The good Lord, in all His wisdom, wouldn't inflict such an epidemic on the entire population of man."

Connor took a minute to absorb what he'd heard. Not sure how to react, he realized Mr. Kelly was joking with him, as he saw the man smile and chuckle.

"Yes, sir, we like turkey hunting, too," Connor said. Connor liked listening to Mr. Kelly. Especially the way he pronounced Tuu-ky, with no "r" sound.

"Turkeys have the unique ability to turn arrogance into hopelessness. The minute you begin to think you have all this business figured out, they are the first to let you know you don't," Tom said with a wide smile.

"Yes, sir, that's the truth. I called my first one by myself the other day. I shot at him but he was too far away. He's probably sitting in a tree somewhere this morning, still laughing at me," Connor said.

"Well, I sure hope they can laugh, because all the things they've seen me do over the last twenty years to amuse them would just be a shameful waste if they didn't," Tom said.

During the conversation, they learned that Mr. Kelly had been a colonel in the army. His accent was interesting. It was southern, but different.

Tom turned to Joe, "Joe, you know the lay of the land here so don't let me get in your way. You tell me where you want me to go and I'll go there. I don't want to interfere with you and the boy's hunt."

"Tom, you're welcome to go anywhere but some of the best hunting is along the southern ridges just up from the creek.

I'll show you a place to try over there. Me and Connor will go to the northern section."

Joe drew directions on a paper napkin with a pencil. He explained to Tom what road to drive from the house to get to the best listening spot.

Tom stuffed the napkin in the pocket of his shirt. "Depending on what happens, I'll probably be back here around nine o'clock. I've got a long drive to Mobile today, so I can't stay and aggravate turkeys too long," Tom said.

"Well, good luck, and we hope to see you then," Joe said. The two men shook hands again.

"Shoot straight, young man," Mr. Kelly slapped Connor's shoulder.

"Yes, sir, I'll try," Connor said.

They finished their farewells; Tom took off in his muddy truck, heading along the old road leading to the southern ridges. Joe drove a long dirt road to get to the northern section before daylight. No wind blew at all.

After Joe parked, they eased a hundred yards along a fireguard ditch, to reach the edge of a large area where the trees had been sawed and hauled away. The clear-cut stretched for hundreds of yards across a hill to the edge of a creek bottom.

"This is a good place to listen and owl," Joe said. "You can hear a turkey gobble a fur piece away over a clear-cut. Only problem with it is, if a turkey is roosted anywhere along the edge, he can see you from a long distance away, so we need to stay hidden back in the trees."

Later, after the morning light had brightened the landscape, Joe hooted like a barred owl. The sound echoed across the open land. A turkey gobbled from their right toward the creek bottom. Connor noticed Joe stoop when he heard the gobble as if crouching to hide.

"He's about three hundred yards across there, probably right on the edge. Let's go back around through the trees until we get down the hill toward the bottom. We'll try to be on the same level as he is," Joe whispered.

They swerved, heading in the direction of the fireguard before turning left into the woods. They eased slowly toward the creek one hundred fifty yards, being careful not to snap any sticks under their feet. They got to the edge of the creek-swamp where the underbrush grew high. Once there, they followed the edge in a slow, careful manner moving toward the clear-cut. When thirty-yards from the edge, they found a place to sit. The tom had not gobbled again. Dawn's shadows lifted to a bright sunny morning.

Joe reached in front of where Connor sat, bending the tops of two bushes in Connor's field of view to the clear-cut's edge. Then Joe settled into a spot close to Connor's left.

When Joe sounded the first cluck, the tom boomed an instant reply. Joe sounded a quick series of yelps before placing the old cedar box on the ground beside him.

The turkey gobbled eight more times during the next three minutes; then, across the open ground in front of them, they saw the big black bird sail out of a tall pine, landing in the clear-cut.

It was visible even at two hundred yards away. When the tom landed, he stood still with his neck stretched high in the air. He took a few steps, pecked at the ground, then went into a full strut. His head tucked tight into his chest, his tail fan expanded wide, with his feathers puffed out as he swiveled slowly to his right, then left.

The big gobbler stayed there for the next hour. Joe called every ten to fifteen minutes. The turkey answered every time but did not come toward them.

Joe whispered to Connor, "This ole turkey is not going to come out of that cutover. He knows all the hens around have a clear view of him out there and he's just waiting on them to come to him."

"What should we do?"

"We have to wait for "him" to do something. If he starts moving, we can try to get ahead of him, but with all this open ground that's gonna be tough. I'll try one more trick to see if I can get him to come over this way."

Joe placed the diaphragm call in his mouth, then picked up the box call. He yelped with both calls at the same time, then made clucks, purrs and more yelps.

To Connor, it sounded like a bunch of turkeys that were upset about something. Joe continued this for two or three minutes.

The turkey ceased his strutting pose, stretched his neck high again, facing their direction before gobbling. He went back into his strut before sashaying back and forth in small circles, the colors in his feathers changing as he pirouetted under the rising sun.

After a few minutes, sharp clucks came from their left under the trees. Three red heads emerged, moving in a line to take them in front of Joe and Connor.

"Wait," whispered Joe.

Connor watched the three turkeys trotting, hopping over toppled trees, clucking all the way. They seemed to be tripping over their own feet while scuttling to find the source of all the turkey talk. Protruding from their chest feathers, Connor saw thick, curly black beards sticking straight out. Each beard, only three inches long.

"Yearling gobblers … jakes," Joe whispered. "Don't shoot."

Connor studied the three comical, long-legged turkeys as their heads bobbed up and down, their necks stretched at a variety of angles, studying the area where Connor sat still. They came so close, Connor saw the sides of their legs well. Little knots formed there, where spurs would eventually grow.

Occasionally, one of the excited birds would spring high in the air, then goose-step a few yards away before continuing its clucking and awkward antics. After a while, the clucks turned into a sound Connor had heard before, an alarm sound his Paw Paw called a *putt*.

He thought back to when Joe said, "That's the sound they make right before they take off running or flying away. That sound warns the turkeys in the area there's danger."

The young toms ran away while making their putt sounds until Connor could no longer hear them. Connor glanced to the clear-cut where the big gobbler had been strutting. The gobbler had long gone.

On the way to the truck, Joe said, "Those three jakes will be gobblers next year and although they're legal to kill now, I'd rather not."

Connor understood. Joe had explained this to Connor before. Joe liked hunting the older birds because they were more of a challenge.

When they returned to Jessie's house at eight-thirty, Mr. Kelly had already arrived. A big gobbler lay on the tailgate of his truck while Mr. Kelly, also sitting on the tailgate, poured coffee from a thermos into a cup.

They examined his bird as Tom told the details of his hunt.

"I was on the way back to the truck about seven-thirty. I hadn't heard squat all morning. I stopped and yelped down a little hollow by the road. He answered from not seventy-five yards away. I didn't have time to make a blind. I just sat down behind a log, propped my gun on top of it and yelped again. He came to me like he was on a string. You just never know what will happen. That turkey was lonesome. He'd probably waited since daylight to get up with his hens and by that time of day, he must have been downright desperate for female company and just committed suicide," Tom said, laughing.

They stayed until the turkey was cleaned. Mr. Kelly insisted that Jessie keep one side of the breast meat.

On the way back to Uriah, Joe and Connor agreed they would like to have more time to visit with Mr. Kelly, and listen to some of his tales.

CHAPTER 23 – WHITE PERCH

Connor and Joe arrived home at eleven-thirty. As soon as they got there, Joe backed the truck up to the boat trailer, hooking it up before he went inside to make lunch.

"Your mama should be here tomorrow after church, so let's straighten up the place while we have time. You wouldn't want her to think I'm makin' you live like a caveman while you was here, would you?" Joe teased.

They ate lunch, swept the floors and quickly tidied up the little house. Then they drove to pick up Janice to go fishing.

When Janice got in the truck in the front seat, in between Joe and Connor, she said, "Oh man, Kenny is so jealous. He loves to fish."

Joe said, "I'll make sure I take him soon. Maybe I'll take him and his brother, too."

The old truck pulled the boat along the county roads to the landing at the river where Joe bought three-dozen live minnows at the bait store, putting them in a bucket full of water. The minnows all went to the bottom, swimming in circles.

"Y'all keep an eye on these minnows today. We'll need to add fresh cool water on them every now and then so they'll stay lively," Joe said.

Joe backed up the boat trailer until the rear end was touching the water in the river. Connor muscled the boat off the trailer and into the water while Joe held the bowline. Joe pulled the boat to the bank until it stuck there, got back in the truck and parked it up the hill.

After he parked the truck, Connor and Janice sat in the boat while Joe pushed the bow off the sandy bank, climbing in.

Joe pulled the rope on the motor as the little Johnson thirty-five cranked, idling smoothly. They motored slowly downstream on the river for a mile, turning right into a wide creek. Along both sides of the creek, tall cypress trees grew with Spanish moss hanging from most of their branches. Around the bottom of each tree trunk, rising above the water, were what Joe had called "cypress knees." The roots grew up out of the water as much as three feet tall in places, standing like wooden statues with smooth round tops.

Joe killed the engine to begin paddling from the back of the boat. He held the paddle directly behind the boat and moved it back and forth making the little boat ease forward silently. Joe called it sculling.

When they came within fifteen feet of the bank, Joe turned, stopping the boat parallel to the bank. He baited the three hooks with live minnows. The minnows wiggled constantly. As soon as they were placed in the water, they quickly swam down into the depths, towing the line behind them until the cork bobber, attached four feet up the line from the hook, stopped their downward progress.

They sat a while, silently watching as the corks floated along between the boat and the bank of the creek.

Joe whispered, "Careful not to slide your feet on the bottom of the boat. These fish are real spooky."

Janice sat beside Connor, watching their lines.

Slowly and steadily, Connor's cork began to sink, "I got one." He lifted the cane fishing pole as the limber end began to dance, bending toward the black water. Connor could feel the fish struggling against his pull. He hoisted the fish out of the depths until it broke the surface, flipped and splashed until it tired. Turning on its side, it lay floating.

Joe gripped the line, hoisting the fish into the boat.

As everyone was busy admiring the shiny scales of the wet fish, Joe suddenly dropped the fish in the bottom of the boat, grabbing his own pole. Another fish had taken his bait while he was distracted with Connor's. As Joe pulled in another fine white perch, Janice screamed, "I got one, too!" as she began wrestling a fish that had taken her bait.

When they all had a fish in the boat, they began removing them from their hooks, untangling lines and celebrating their luck. Joe said, "When you get into 'em, it can be fast action. Stay calm and just lift the pole up, slow and steady. Don't pull up too hard or the hook will tear out of their mouth. Then, you'll lose the fish. You have to be gentle but keep your line tight all the time."

Then he winked to Janice, "I do believe you might be a good luck charm, young lady."

Janice smiled, turning to scoop another minnow for her hook.

The afternoon sun became warm as they sculled along the creek, catching white perch, drinking cold bottles of Coca-Cola that Joe had packed in a bag of ice.

As the sun began to get lower in the sky, they pulled in the lines. Joe cranked the engine to head back to the landing. Connor and Janice crouched over the fish-well located under the center seat of the boat, trying to count the fish swimming around inside it as the boat motored down the river. They estimated they had caught more than twenty. Some of them would weigh over a pound. The fish would make several fine meals for their families.

Back at the landing, after the boat was loaded on the trailer, Janice noticed a man shuffling down the hill toward their boat. It was Mr. Hudson, the catfish man.

"Hey, Mr. Hudson," Janice waved as the man came close.

The man wore a dirty undershirt, the kind that exposed the shoulders, with a pair of sagging blue work pants. His belly hung over his belt and the black stubble of his beard partially hid a weathered face. His white rubber boots flopped with each step. He held a can of beer in one hand and a cigarette in the other.

"Hey there, young lady. Y'all catch any today?" he said.

"Yes, sir," she replied. "Kenny has some crawdads for you. We caught them earlier this week."

"Oh, good. Just drop them by anytime."

The man shook Joe's hand, speaking in familiar tones. It was obvious to Connor they knew each other.

He put the cigarette in the corner of his mouth. When he spoke, it bounced up and down, "Joe, I heard a turkey gobble this morning while I was pullin' lines down by Miller's Creek. There's a big high ridge that runs along up there an' he was up on that high ground, right at daylight. I figured you'd wanna know. I seen your truck down here an' thought I'd walk down the hill an' tell ya."

"Much obliged, John. That's good to know. We went all the way to Beatrice this morning hoping to kill one, but came back without him," Joe said.

Connor wondered if Paw Paw ever went turkey hunting in his boat.

What an adventure that would be.

As they bumped along the road leading away from Eureka Landing, Connor noticed the shabby houses along the way. Some of their low porches sagged down, almost to the ground. Several front yards were filled with large groups of Negros.

They all seemed to be having a good time. Some of the men sat under shade trees in old wooden chairs while children were running and playing everywhere.

Connor knew this was one of many Negro neighborhoods scattered around the county. Most of the men were either saw-hands on logging crews or were unemployed. On Saturday afternoons, they gathered in front yards for weekly socializing with their neighbors. Some of the men stared as the truck passed by, while a few men waved.

They drove to Janice's house. Mr. Johnson was told about the fish they had caught. Joe promised to bring some to him after he'd cleaned them. Mr. Johnson protested that he would be glad to clean the fish himself but Joe insisted on doing it. Mr. Johnson thanked him.

Back home, Joe and Connor cleaned and scaled twenty-three white perch, wrapped the meat in freezer paper, divided the meat into five large packs, then put one pack in the freezer. They placed the other four packs of meat in the refrigerator to take to the Johnsons tomorrow after church.

Joe knew how to handle the division of the fish. If he'd let Mr. Johnson divide the fish before they were cleaned, then the Johnsons would insist that they only take half. This way, as far as the Johnsons knew, four packs of fish *were* half the catch.

Connor began to understand how Joe operated.
Paw Paw is smart. Like an old tom turkey.
Connor was exhausted that night from the busiest day of fun he'd had since he'd arrived. He fell asleep as his head touched the pillow.

Chapter 24 – Silver Cross

Both Joe and Connor had decided they would skip hunting this morning. They needed to rest. The last week of hunting every morning had worn them down. Sunday, it was decided, was a good day to get a little extra sleep. Joe had decided that since Connor had to attend school Monday, doing so in a state of "worn slap out" was not the best idea.

When Connor rose from bed, it was seven-thirty. It felt good to stay in bed for a change but he still missed hunting.

At church, Connor was invited to sit with the Johnson family. Janice sat beside her father while Connor sat on her other side. They shared a hymnal during each song, and Connor noticed Janice had a beautiful signing voice. Connor mouthed the words but mostly listened to her. Janice wasn't shy when it came to singing or anything else for that matter. She had a quiet but solid air of confidence about her, even at such a tender age. Connor already admired the fact that she wasn't embarrassed or ashamed to be herself. This made Connor want to be like her.

At one point during a hymn, he whispered to her, "Can you go to the creek today?"

"I think so, what time?"

"Maybe around three?"

"I'll try," she whispered back.

After church, as soon as Joe finished shaking the preacher's hand at the front door, a young man approached Joe, "Mr. Parker, I still haven't killed that ole turkey."

"Is that so?" Joe said.

"I tried the tricks you told me about but I ended up scaring him off. Do you think you could go with me one morning this week and we could give him a try?"

Joe smiled at the young man, "I'd like that. Sure, let's plan on Tuesday if the weather's good. I'll meet you at the café at five." With that, the young man shook Joe's hand, thanking him.

Later, Connor queried Joe about the man. Joe said, "The young feller's name is Daniel Myers," and explained the situation.

Connor felt a pang of jealousy at Paw Paw hunting with somebody else, while at the same time, Connor felt proud of his Paw Paw. Not only for having a reputation as a good turkey hunter but for being the type of man who made people feel at ease if they asked for help.

When they arrived home, Nancy was already there. Connor noticed she had brought his bicycle with her. It was tied to the roof of the station wagon. Connor had only had the bike a year. The "spider" style bike sported a "banana" seat with high handlebars and knobby tires. They unloaded the bike from the roof after exchanging tight hugs.

Nancy spoke to them both, "I'm sorry I had to work yesterday, but it's tax season and the workload is pretty intense. I really had to beg to take two vacation days this week."

Joe spoke up, "How's that job going? You still moving up the ladder there?"

"Daddy, it's not going well. They promoted Jim Rodgers two weeks ago, and I have three more years at the company than he has and I produce more work. They always promote the men first. That's just the way it is."

"That ain't right. You should be judged on the work you do, not whether you're male or female. I don't see how a man would have any advantage in book-work over a woman."

"It's always been that way, Daddy. I'd love to work at a place where my work was what mattered most but I don't think that's possible."

"Well, come on in, I've got some peas ready to go in the pressure cooker and I'll bake some fresh cornbread while you and Connor settle in and catch up."

Connor and his mother talked about the last week. Since they'd been apart, Connor stayed busy but still missed his mom. It was good to have her here with him.

~~~~~~~

Since Connor had been away for a week, Nancy had been alone in the house. She missed him intensely. The house was empty. She felt lonely and sad all week. She didn't speak a word of her feelings to Connor. She didn't want him to feel guilty about living with his Paw Paw. Nancy still felt the pain of losing her husband and this week, without Connor, was especially hard.

After they ate the pink-eyed purple-hulled peas, cornbread and link sausage, they relaxed on the front porch. The dogwoods under the pines beyond the front yard had begun to bloom. A light breeze made the porch shade chilly.

"We'll need to get you registered in the school first thing in the morning before the first bell," Nancy said. "Maybe we can finish with that so you can make it to homeroom by eight. You have all your school supplies ready to go?"

"Yes, ma'am, I'm ready," Connor said. "Can we find out about tryouts in the morning?"

"Sure, we'll ask but I want you to concentrate on school work more than baseball, okay?"

"Yes, ma'am."

Joe inquired, "Is there anything you'd like me to do?"

"I think we'll be okay, Daddy," Nancy said, handing Connor a small white box, "Here, see what you think of this."

Connor opened the box to see a silver necklace with a cross that hung from the chain.

"I think I got my first necklace like that when I was around fourteen. This one was on sale for five dollars, so pay up, young man." She poked him.

"Yes, ma'am, I think she'll like it a lot," Connor said. He went inside to get the ten-dollar bill he'd stored in his bedroom.

When he returned, he said, "Are you going hunting in the morning, Paw Paw?"

"Well, if y'all are sure I'm not needed, I might go listen a while," Joe said. "I'll be here when you get out of school. I suppose you'll want to take the bus home."

"Yes, sir. Where you going to listen?"

"I was thinking of taking the boat and going down to that ridge where John heard one. I'd like to check out that area. I'll let you know all about it tomorrow afternoon. Meanwhile, we can get some lines ready today and I'll put them out in the creek for catfish before daylight and check them when I get through hunting. Might pick up a few fish while I'm there."

Quickly, Connor responded, "I can go catch a few crawdads for bait this afternoon."

"If you can catch about a dozen, that's all I can use."

Connor found an empty bucket in the barn before riding his bike to the creek.

CHAPTER 25 –FIRST TIME

Connor lay the bicycle down beside the road when he got to the creek. He went down the trail, took off his shoes, and waded into the creek. He caught two crawfish before Janice arrived. When she spied Connor, she said. "Whew, I'm glad it's you. I didn't know you had a bicycle. Wasn't sure who was down here."

"Hey. Yeah, my mom brought it with her today. What's your brothers up to?"

"They're going to the landing with Daddy to sell those crawfish," she said. "Caught any yet?"

"Two," he said. He offered his hand as she stepped down the bank to enter the creek.

They spent the next hour in the creek, eventually catching a dozen crawdads. A half-submerged log lay across it. They sat on it to rest.

As they talked, Connor gathered his courage, putting his arm around her shoulders, "I can't wait 'till your birthday."

"Really?"

"Yeah, I got you something and I hope you like it."

"What is it?" She giggled.

"Gotta wait. Not gonna tell ya."

Janice turned to Connor, leaned forward and kissed him quickly on the lips. Connor was astonished but tried to conceal his surprise. Nothing was said for a long while as they stared down into the creek, content to watch the water flow around their feet.

On the way home, it became a struggle for Connor to carry the bucket, half-full of water and crawdads, as it hung from the left handlebar. Several times, while pedaling the bike, his knee bumped the bucket, throwing the bike off balance. He didn't want to spill the bucket in the middle of the clay road. It took a while to pedal back home, especially when the way home was steadily uphill.

He sat the bucket on the front porch on his way inside. Nancy and Joe, with cups of fresh coffee, watched a news report on television. Walter Cronkite talked with Henry Kissinger about the war in Viet Nam. It seemed to Connor like all he'd ever seen on the news was Viet Nam. He wondered if the war would ever end. He worried he'd have to go fight when he reached eighteen. Maybe he would be drafted or have to join the army.

He interrupted, "Paw Paw, did you ever go in the military?"

"No, when I went for the physical, they discovered I had a hernia and said I couldn't join," Joe said. "I went to work for the power company shortly after that."

The next question came out of Connor's mouth before he could stop it. "Mama, when was the first time you ever kissed a boy?"

Nancy stared at Connor with her eyebrows raised, "None of your business, young man."

Joe glanced at Nancy, winked, and quickly changed the subject.

"Connor, let's hook up the boat trailer. I'd rather do it now than to have to do it in the dark in the morning."

Outside, the sun was sinking as the birds were noisily feeding around the yard. A fox squirrel scampered away.

"Whoa, look at that," Connor said pointing at the big red squirrel.

Joe chuckled, "That joker eats a lot of my pecans. But I can't bring myself to shoot him. He's too pretty. And there's not many fox squirrels left. Same as quail. They're disappearing."

They hooked the boat trailer to the truck, closed the gate to the chicken pen, and went inside for the night.

As he lay down that night, he wished his mom could live here, too. Tomorrow carried the promise of new faces, with a completely new experience for Connor.

CHAPTER 26 – BLACKSHER HIGH

When Connor and Nancy parked in front of the school at seven AM on Monday, kids unloaded from the buses. Connor noticed he didn't see any colored kids at all.

They shuffled into the school office. While Nancy completed the paperwork, Connor studied the display of sports trophies in the lobby. Two regional baseball championship trophies were displayed in the middle, larger than any of the other awards.

A colored girl, carrying a pile of papers, strolled into the lobby, launching a curious grin at Connor. "Who is you?" she said without hesitation.

Connor had seldom spoken with colored people before. He hesitated, speaking softly, "My name's Connor. This is my first day."

She giggled, "Lawd, lawd. Ain't you sumpin. I'm Pawleen. You let me know if you need anythang. I knows errybody up in dis place." She laid the papers on a desk, making her exit without another word.

Connor stood with both hands in his pockets. His eyes followed the big girl as she maneuvered through the door. Not sure how to react, he glanced around the room to see if anyone else had witnessed the greeting or could offer any clue as to what protocol may be. Bewildered, he just smiled.

Well, that was weird. But ... it was nice.

Connor learned later that day that only three Negros had come to the school. They were all female.

The assistant principal, Mrs. Thompson, came out into the lobby handing Connor a piece of paper. "Here's your schedule, Connor. Come on, I'll show you to your homeroom."

Connor waved to his mom through the glass separating the office from the lobby as they left. As they strolled, Mrs. Thompson explained how the classrooms were numbered. She pointed the way to the gymnasium. When they reached the homeroom door, she swung it open, gave the teacher the piece of paper, then left.

Connor studied the room.

The opening bell had not yet rung so several kids stood together talking. Others sat at their desks fumbling with papers and books. He took a seat in the first row of desks, second to the front by the wall.

The bell rang as a tall boy behind him punched his shoulder with his finger.

Connor spun around in his desk.

The boy reached out his hand, fingers upward, palm open.

Connor clenched his hand. A modern handshake was exchanged.

"Bobby Hadley," he said.

"Connor McCoy."

The boy leaned back in his desk. "Cool."

Connor hoped meeting people here would continue to be that easy.

The teacher called the roll. She called Connor's name last.

"Here," Connor responded.

The teacher said, "Welcome, Connor, I'm Mrs. Hall."

Connor began his first day at J.U. Blacksher High School, home of the Bulldogs.

CHAPTER 27 – JUST IN TIME

Joe killed the boat's engine, letting the boat drift with the current in the middle of Rhodes Creek, which flowed southwest to the Alabama River. He reached into a large canvas bag, retrieving a large mason jar, painted white, containing two feet of stout cord. The cord would be taken out then, screwing the lid tight on one end of the cord, while the other end would go in the water. The line held a lead weight above a large silver hook at the end.

He uncovered the bucket, reaching inside to grip a crawfish. Next he slid the sharp hook though the crawdad's tough shell. Joe dropped the first jar over the side before grabbing another.

When he had dropped all the jars into the water, Joe glanced behind him. Without any wind to propel the floating jars across the surface, reflecting the bright light of a half moon, they floated in a line for a hundred yards along the middle of Rhodes Creek.

Joe pulled the engine's cranking rope. The little engine pushed the boat another three-quarter mile upstream in the creek as it peeled off more to the south. Joe cut the engine, peering in the direction of the high ridge to his right. He rested the paddle on the stern, waiting. Though dark, the moon created enough light to see around him. He propped the paddle inside the boat before pouring a hot cup of coffee from the thermos. Water birds occasionally disturbed the quiet scene with their piercing squawk. Bullfrogs croaked everywhere along the river bottom, their deep, guttural sounds echoing over the water. Mosquitoes swirled around Joe's head, buzzing and biting.

He grabbed a can of repellent to spray his hat and hands. While wiping the lotion into his face, ears and neck, a bass struck the water at the edge of the creek in a patch of lily pads as the boat sat silent, drifting in the dark water.

When daylight broke, owls called from every direction. Joe sculled the boat at a slow pace while listening for a gobble. From far ahead of the boat farther downstream in the creek, he caught a faint gobble. He put both hands behind his ears, cupping them in the direction of the sound. It sounded so far away, all he could hear was what sounded like someone whispering "Yaw." He sculled with more force, driving the boat forward.

When he'd traveled another hundred yards up the creek, the sound became more distinct. It came from high on the ridge to his right. He slowed the boat to a silent crawl toward the right-hand bank, scouting all the while for an opening to land the boat between the cypress knees.

The turkey gobbled as if it were a Siren's song, leading sailors onto the rocks. When the boat scraped the bank, Joe scooted forward, catching a low-hanging limb and tying the bow rope to it. He stepped onto the bank with his shotgun hanging from a makeshift leather sling on his left shoulder. After prowling a few steps into the soggy river bottom, he stopped to listen again. Saw palmettos shaded the floor of the forest, growing as high as three feet tall. The turkey gobbled again. Joe ascended the hillside with care toward the top, where the tom beckoned.

Halfway up the tall hill, the ground leveled for two-dozen yards, creating a shelf. As Joe crept across this flat part of his climb, he detected the leaves on the ground had been disturbed. This pattern signaled this as turkey "scratching sign." The scratching occupied a broad area on the shelf. He jotted a mental note.

This is their strut zone. When a gobbler wants to strut, and attract a hen, he likes a place that's open and flat. This shelf is perfect for that.

He considered setting up there to call the turkey, but decided to move forward, climbing to try to get closer to the noisy bird.

Near the top of the ridge, he eased up to peek over the rim. The ridge top lay flat. It had recently been logged, leaving a cutover dropping off the other side where, Joe assumed, the log trucks had come into the area from a road.

Joe reasoned the gobbler waited in the cutover, gobbling to summon his harem, moving back and forth in the clearing, gobbling his heart out. Joe dared not move any closer to try to get a look at the bird for fear it might see him. He sat, placing his back against a large water oak. He sat twenty yards from the cutover edge, watching uphill. If a turkey strolled across the edge, Joe could see him silhouetted against the morning sky.

Joe called with two clucks. The tom answered. Two gobbles back to back with hardly time for a breath between, showing his enthusiasm. He continued to gobble regularly at every sound he heard but would not exit the cutover. After an hour, he quit gobbling. Joe crawled up the hill, peering into the clear-cut area. Far to the left, on the other side of a low spot in the open ground, a large hen stood silhouetted against the sky. She ambled to his left, abandoning the open area. Two gobblers followed behind the hen, with an occasional pause to strut. He studied their behavior until the three turkeys waddled from sight.

Unfamiliar with the lay of the land, Joe figured he had no chance to get in front of them to cut them off. Besides, the terrain here had already exhausted him. He had made quite a long climb up the hill earlier.

Joe descended the hill to the shelf he passed earlier. He lay against a huge log, resting his head on it. He called a long series of yelps before pulling his hat down over his eyes to take a nap. Every thirty minutes or so, he raised his head, slowly surveying his surroundings, listening before yelping again. He repeated the process for two hours while drifting in and out of a light sleep.

Joe decided to give up. He wanted to return to his catfish lines before the wind picked up. The wind could push the lines into the creek banks, making retrieval difficult. He sauntered down the hill to get to the boat before untying the line from the tree limb. As he stepped into the boat, a turkey gobbled halfway up the hill. Joe knew the tom had come to the strut zone wondering where the loud hen he'd been listening to all morning had gone.

Joe laughed aloud, shaking his head.

Well, I left just in time.

He plopped down on the seat to crank the engine.

When he spied the first jar, it had moved to the side of the creek but not too close to the bank. He kept an eye on the jar for any sign of movement. He slid the boat alongside it. As the boat idled past, he snatched it. After pulling the line into the boat, he found no bait, leaving a bare silver hook.

The next jar he spotted moved upstream in the middle of the creek. When the boat slid near, he put the engine in neutral, moving to the edge of the boat while kneeling on both knees. He scooped up the jar. The fish pulled against his grip but he kept the line taut before hoisting the fish into the boat. The fish flopped against the aluminum boat floor, causing quite a racket. He estimated the catfish weighed two pounds; just right for the frying pan.

Joe eventually retrieved the twelfth line; he had five catfish in the fish-well under the middle seat.

After returning home, he skinned the fish, wrapping the meat for the freezer. Joe sat on the porch with Nancy, who asked about the hunt. Questions Joe considered courtesy more than curiosity or much real interest. Joe told a short account of the hunt before inquiring how registration went at school.

"Everything went fine, Daddy. I met the principal and the assistant principal. Everyone seemed very nice. The school is clean. The kids seem happy to be there. I hope Connor fits in here and makes some new friends. At fourteen, it may be hard."

She crossed her arms, looking out over the yard, "I miss Connor more than I thought I would, Daddy," she confided. "I've been thinking of changing jobs. If Connor does well here, I may try to find a job in Monroeville or Atmore."

Joe's eyes brightened as he turned to his daughter, "You mean you would actually consider moving back up here?"

"Let's see how Connor does. And what my boss does after this tax season is over. I've been thinking about it. I'm just not sure yet."

"I see. Well, you know what I'll be hoping for. But whatever you decide, I trust it will be the right decision for you and Connor."

"I really appreciate you taking Connor in like this. He is enjoying it. Makes me a little jealous," she said with a laugh.

"Connor misses you, too, Nancy. I can tell he does. I'll take care of him the best I can, but I'll never replace you or his father. You know that."

"I know, Daddy, I know."

~~~~~~~

After supper, Nancy left the home where she had been raised. With the windows rolled down, she breathed in the familiar spring air as the station wagon turned from the driveway. She noticed the trees, budding green sprouts. The dogwoods in bloom. Memories flooded her mind of her childhood on the little farm, the dirt roads, the fields and her old friends from school. The money from James' life insurance would make it easier for her to take a cut in pay. She considered if she could sell the house in Mobile. Finances were not a factor in the decision to move.

So, what is holding me back?

CHAPTER 28 – THE ABSOLUTE TRUTH

It pleased Connor to learn most of the classes were in subjects he had studied in Mobile. This kept him even with his classmates when it came to schoolwork.

He found it easy to change from one class to the other, locating the right rooms. During lunch, Janice introduced him to her best friend Cheryl. He met several other students during the day.

At lunch, Janice pointed out the coach. Connor approached him, introducing himself. He learned the coach held baseball practice on Tuesdays and Thursdays after school, then asked if he could try out.

The coach said, "Come prepared to try out tomorrow. I'll see what you've got."

Connor smacked his hands together, relieved to know his glove and cleats waited at Paw Paw's house.

Later, Connor strolled to his locker with textbooks. The lockers were located against the hallway walls. The school required him to provide his own combination lock for his locker. The office secretary had told him the local hardware store carried locks.

He left the books he didn't need to take home in his locker. Nobody wanted to steal textbooks, but he'd get a lock later in case he had to store anything valuable there.

Janice had told him which bus to board after school. They met before getting on the bus together. The bus filled with noisy students. Connor and Janice discussed the day until the bus stopped in front of Joe Parker's house to let Connor off. Connor wondered how the bus driver knew where to stop. He had been too busy talking to Janice to think about telling the driver himself.

After Joe told Connor the details of the morning hunt and cat fishing, he said, "Well, what do you think of the school?"

"It's okay. It's different there. Everybody knows everybody," Connor said. He sat at the kitchen table to work on homework assignments.

After finishing his homework, Connor helped his grandpa stake the tomato plants with the canes they had cut earlier. Connor drove each cane deep in the ground at least four inches away from each plant to avoid damaging their tiny roots.

Joe explained, "These plants will get up around four or five feet tall. When they're full of tomatoes, they'll be heavy. So, the stakes should be driven deep so they'll be strong. A big wind can knock over the plants. We don't want that. It damages the stems and the tomatoes won't grow anymore."

Connor was learning much about gardening, turkey hunting, crawfish catching and country life in the short time he'd been there. He found the long conversations about wildlife with Paw Paw interesting. Connor soaked it in, yearning for a real connection to this lifestyle.

"Paw Paw, did Mr. Kelly go to college to learn how to be a forestry boss?"

Connor thought that someday he might like to have a job like that. The thought of working in the woods every day, instead of inside an office was appealing.

"Jessie told me he went to Auburn to study forestry. Back then it was called Alabama Polytechnic Institute."

"Really? They have a degree in that?"

Neat.

"Yep, Auburn has all kinds of programs for farming, animal medicine, forestry, and wildlife."

Connor considered a degree in something to do with wildlife. The idea excited him. He decided he would gather all the information he could about these programs before he graduated from high school.

Joe told Connor he'd pick him up after baseball practice the next afternoon.

"I hope you can help Daniel kill that turkey in the morning, Paw Paw. I wish I could go," Connor said.

"All we can do is see what the situation is and do our best. Ain't no guarantees with turkeys, buddy."

"Yes, sir. That's the truth ... that's the absolute truth."

CHAPTER 29 – IT TAKES TWO

The café had yet to open when Daniel Myers met Joe. Joe got in Daniel's truck to head toward Little River, which ran several miles to the south.

When they penetrated the woods, they hiked to the edge of a gas line running through Daniel's family land. They stopped on the top of a hill.

Daniel pointed down the hill to their right along the gas line, as they stood in the dark, "He always roosts down in that hollow. Sometimes, he shows himself along the gas line and sometimes he comes out right here from across the clearing. Either way, he hangs up about eighty yards away. He won't come any closer."

The gas line clearing lay thirty yards wide. Joe assessed the situation, whispering, "This tom may have come to a hunter's call before. He saw a hunter or maybe he's even been shot at before. Regardless, he's one of those who won't come to a call unless he sees a hen."

Joe pointed to a large tree at the edge of the clearing, "Build a blind in front of you and sit right there. I'm going down the hill to our left and sit about eighty yards away down there. I'll call about every fifteen or twenty minutes. Let's see if he'll come to this point before he hangs up. Maybe you can get a shot at him on his way to my calling. It may take a while, so just sit tight right here."

Joe eased down the hill to find a place to sit.

Daniel stayed on the edge of the gas line, trimming and arranging bushes to construct a makeshift blind before settling behind it.

I've got the roosting area downhill to my right and Mr. Parker downhill to my left. This might work.

At daylight, Joe yelped. The hill lay between Joe and the place where the turkey usually roosted. Joe listened. Nothing responded to his call.

After one hour, without hearing a turkey gobble, Joe had little hope anything was going to happen but decided to continue calling occasionally for another thirty minutes.

Daniel's shotgun blast startled Joe. He rose to scale the hill. Daniel stood over a gobbler, dead on the ground.

"Did he come without gobbling?" Joe said with a smile.

Daniels eyes were wide, "No, sir. He gobbled all the way up here. You didn't hear him? He gobbled his head off."

"I didn't hear a thing from down there in that hollow," Joe said. "It's amazing how this little hill blocked all that sound."

With a wide smile, Daniel replied, "Well, the plan worked like a charm. He gobbled from the roost for an hour before he finally flew off the roost and came walkin' down the gas line, just like he's done several times before. But this time, he went trucking right past me going to you. He didn't know what hit him."

"Sometimes with a tom like this one, it takes two people to kill him. I'm glad it all worked out but I sure wish I could've heard him. I was about to give up," Joe said.

Daniel hoisted the turkey to his shoulder.

Joe said, "Hey, ain't this April the first?"

"Yes, sir, I believe it is."

"Hmm, I reckon we played an April fool's joke on him."

They ambled back to the truck, dropping the turkey in the back.

144

"Breakfast is on me, Mr. Joe," Daniel declared.

"That'll be fine," Joe said.

On the way to the café, Daniel told Joe all the details of previous mornings, how each time he'd failed to get a shot at the turkey.

Daniel's rapid speech, coupled with exaggerated hand gestures, assured Joe that Daniel was one of those rare young men who welcomed the challenge of turkey hunting and found the competition fascinating.

At the café, several men from the community ate inside. Daniel praised Joe for the hunt's success. Joe sat in silence, enjoying Daniel repeating the story of the hard-to-kill ole turkey.

CHAPTER 30 – THE TRYOUT

Connor stepped on the baseball field at three-thirty. The players warmed up, throwing to one another while a few stretched. The coach summoned them to the area outside the bullpen. They formed a semicircle around him.

"We're going to practice in the field today, and then take some batting practice. We have a transfer student today. This is Connor McCoy." He pointed to Connor, "Y'all introduce yourselves. He'll be moving around the field today. Good luck, Connor."

Several of the players repeated the coach saying, "Good luck, man." One slapped him on the back with a glove. The team spirit encouraged Connor, reinforcing his desire to join the team.

The coach barked his orders, "Take your field positions. Tom, get a bat." A boy with jet-black hair topping his ears, grabbed a bat. The rest of the team took the field. Several extra players waited in the outfield. Kenny Johnson, with his catcher's mitt, trotted to home plate.

Very few boys at this school had hair covering the top of their ears. Connor wondered if Tom bucked the system with bravado or was just too poor to get a haircut. The baseball cap made it hard to tell if his hair was styled that way or if it grew wild under there.

Connor watched the coach for instructions. "Get behind the shortstop, we'll let you alternate on grounders a while," Coach said.

Connor ran full speed to his position.

The first grounder Tom hit to Connor bounced hard as a high-hopper. Connor rushed toward the ball, meeting it at the edge of the infield grass, taking it in his glove at the level of his chest. Both hands met the ball as Connor fluidly retrieved the ball from the glove with his throwing-hand at eye level while still moving forward; he fired a shot to first base. The ball popped like a gunshot when it struck the first baseman's mitt.

"Good shot," came from the second baseman. The third baseman said, "Good arm, Connor."

During the afternoon practice, Connor played shortstop as well as fielding fly balls in the outfield. Once, he showed his speed when a fly ball flew down the line, allowing Connor to make the catch, running at full speed.

Batting practice consisted of ten pitches to each player. Each took a turn at the plate. The pitches were medium speed, down the middle, allowing the batters to work on their swings.

Connor slapped several hot grounders. The infielders found several of his hot-shots too hard to field. Connor's long, wiry arms and taut muscles made his swing powerful.

By the time practice ended, most of the other players joked with Connor, acting excited to have him on their team, even though the coach had not made it official yet.

The coach ordered the team to run sprints from home plate to the center field fence, then sprint back. As they cleaned up the field, the coach spoke again to everybody. "Work on your swings, guys. Turn your hips and swing level. That's all it takes. Oh, and one more thing, Tom, get that hair cut this week."

Several loud "yes, sirs" came from the players. As the coach turned toward the locker room, he glanced at Connor, "McCoy, you're in. Be here Thursday. Same time."

"Yes, sir." Connor struggled to contain his excitement. He formed a fist, smashing his glove several times as he left the field.

I'm in! Hot damn, I'm in.

Connor ran to Joe's truck waiting in the parking area, opening the passenger door. "I got in, Paw Paw. Let's go home and call Mom."

"That's good. Where's your books, son?"

"Aw, heck, I left them in the dugout. I'll be right back."

~~~~~~

Joe watched the boy run back to the field, while he reflected on his own days playing ball when younger.

That feeling never changes from generation to generation.

Connor jabbered all the way home, telling Joe about every play he'd pulled in detail. Joe never told Connor he'd been watching him the entire time from a secluded place behind the bleachers on the third base side of the field.

Joe just listened, letting the boy talk. Hearing the excitement in his voice was almost as good as watching his grandson play with such confidence.

CHAPTER 31 – THE SCHEME

The next morning, Joe stayed home, seeing Connor off to school. He phoned his old friend Jessie Pickens at his office in Monroeville. The office had been there for the last thirty-five years. He always came to work by seven.

"I need to meet with you, if you have time this week, Jessie," Joe said.

"I've got to come through Uriah later this morning, Joe. How 'bout a cup of coffee at the café around eleven?" Jessie replied.

Joe agreed.

He spent the morning on the tractor mowing weeds on the trails behind his field, tending to the chicken pen and checking the condition of the vegetable garden.

He arrived at the café just before eleven AM, waiting for Jessie to arrive. As Jessie sat at a table in the back of the café, which only had room for two people, Mr. and Mrs. Brunson came in for an early lunch.

The pair attended church with Joe. If he had arrived at the café after they had taken a seat, he would have felt obligated to sit with them or apologize, explaining he was to meet someone. Joe was happy to avoid that.

Five years ago, Joe had made the mistake of sitting with them during a meal. Cheryl Brunson loved to talk—she loved to talk a lot. It didn't seem to matter to her whether she had her mouth full of food when the urge to talk hit her. Joe did not tolerate bad table manners well. Watching her chew while talking for thirty minutes had caused Joe's stomach great distress. He did not wish to repeat the experience. Potluck dinners at church had since required a strategic effort to find a seat somewhere away from Mrs. Brunson. Today, he would not have to suffer the ordeal. He smiled.

Dodged that bullet.

Jessie entered, strolling to the table to sit. The two men engaged in niceties, catching up on news from one another's families. Joe didn't wait long to get to the point.

"Jessie, I may have an idea for you about replacing Mrs. Baker. Now, don't think I'm asking for a favor because I'm not. I would like for you to consider talking to Nancy about the job. It's your decision on who you hire. I'm not even sure that Nancy is interested in the job, but I wanted to speak to you first before I mentioned it to her."

"I'd be glad to talk to her, Joe, but it's really going to be up to Mrs. Baker who we hire. She knows a lot more about what we need than I do. She wants to train a person she thinks will do a good job and stay there a while," Jessie said. "I'll mention it to her. I'm sure she'll be glad to talk to her, if Nancy's interested, that is."

"That's all I'm asking. If Nancy is interested, I'll tell her to call Mrs. Baker and whatever happens, happens."

"Good enough," Jessie said. "Now how's the boy? Did he get on the baseball team yet?"

Joe and Jessie finished their coffee before each went his separate way. Before exiting the restaurant, Joe spoke to the Brunsons out of courtesy but gazed out the window while they talked.

~~~~~~

At school, Connor continued to learn more about the culture in Uriah. He learned why the team didn't practice on

Wednesdays. All the churches held prayer meetings every Wednesday night. Even though kids seldom attended, no coach in his right mind would schedule practice on Wednesday evenings, risking scorn for interfering with church.

He also discovered that most of the kids in school had known one another since the first grade, with many being kin or at least having family connections to one another. Connor marveled at the social structure here, yet experienced a twinge of jealousy that he had missed out on this close community during his younger years.

Connor and Janice ate lunch in the school cafeteria every day, along with various friends, at the same long table. He didn't mind the food but the students always complained. It became a way to be cool, so he joined in whenever the opportunity arose.

CHAPTER 32 – JONES BLUFF

Joe didn't usually miss a morning of turkey hunting other than an occasional Sunday or an extremely rainy day during the short spring seasons. Yesterday, however, he wanted to ring Jessie early, while he knew Jessie was still in the office, so he'd made the sacrifice. Today, he rose again at four AM without the benefit of the alarm.

Joe wrapped sausage biscuits in foil for Connor to warm for breakfast. Connor would catch the bus to go to school later. Joe always felt a twinge of guilt for abandoning the boy at home.

He drove to Jones Bluff to hunt the turkey that had been hard to call. When he arrived on the hill where he usually stopped to listen, he kept hiking. He entered the hollow below, in the direction where the turkey gobbled during the last hunt there. When he got close to the wet center of the wide hollow, daylight crept into the canopy.

The dense trees overhead caused most ground vegetation to grow low and sparse. Only dark-green ferns with wide leaves grew in patches all around Joe. He found a place beside a large cottonwood tree, settling in to wait.

The owls called to one another across the wide, damp hollow. Joe hoped he would be able to hear the turkey gobble from this low in the swamp.

Joe leaned his head against the bark of the tree trunk. He closed his eyes, listening close. He decided he wouldn't produce a sound until the tom gobbled first. The songbirds woke, chirping while flitting about. The flutter of their wings swirled the air as some flew close to him. The owls quit calling as daylight grew. A few crows cawed on the hills above him. Joe continued to linger. He had nothing on his agenda today, with nowhere to be until Connor got out of school later this afternoon. Joe owned the day. It filled him with contentment here, sitting in the middle of the woods he loved. He became as much a part of the scene as an old pine stump, taking in the sounds of the wild morning forest.

The sun had penetrated through the canopy of trees before a turkey made a sound. A hen cut loud from a hundred yards to the left along the wide hollow. When the hen stopped, a tom gobbled through the hollow to Joe's right. Joe raised the gun onto his knee, picking up the cedar box call. The tom didn't gobble again. Joe waited a while before he made two clucks, setting the call down while scanning the surrounding area with his eyes.

The turkey remained silent. Joe gave him another fifteen minutes, remaining motionless.

The brush rustled over his right shoulder. Then another *swoosh*. The tom dragged his wings along the ground, brushing the green ferns with them as he eased along. Joe's head turned inch-by-inch to his right, keeping the back of his head firm against the tree trunk. He turned his eyes to the right until they hurt, trying to peer in that direction without moving.

Twenty yards to Joe's right, the gobbler came into view. The turkey moved slowly, his blue and red head investigating the area with its eyes. Joe could only freeze, hoping the turkey came around in front of him. He had no way to shoot to his right before the bird would spook into a run. Joe gasped shallow breaths to avoid causing any movement in his torso but his heart thundered in his chest.

The turkey eased ahead, presenting Joe with a better view. He wore a thick, heavy beard and moved cautiously through the ferns. Joe noticed the tom's demeanor transform. The big tom flipped his wing feathers slightly as they lay against his body. His head rose while his left eye, the only one that Joe could see, locked onto Joe. In a flash the turkey spun, sounding a loud, sharp putt before running in the direction he had come. Joe had been seen somehow, although he hadn't batted an eye.

Joe breathed out in a heavy sigh, relaxing the tense muscles in his legs and arms. He sat still until his heart stopped pounding, then rose to hike to the truck. All the way, he wondered if he had moved or done anything to cause the turkey to see him. He decided there was nothing he could have done differently. The tom recognized that Joe, sitting in the woods, formed an unfamiliar shape. The wise bird decided something wasn't right.

Joe's frustration subsided with the prospect of the next battle of wits with the gobbler. Joe smiled, thankful he had gotten close to him.

He stopped for coffee at the café. The Methodist preacher, with his wife, exited as Joe parked the truck. They spoke for a while, reminding Joe about the upcoming Easter service, combining all the churches in the community.

The preacher said, "I hear that grandson of yours is quite a ball player."

Joe deduced the coach, one of the Methodists, had mentioned Connor to his pastor. "Well, I hope he does his part for the team."

Easter, only a few days away, meant Connor would be out of school for Good Friday, tomorrow. Nancy planned to visit again on Saturday. Joe expected to enjoy the long weekend.

Over coffee, Joe spoke with the farmers about the weather, along with the usual subjects discussed in the small café most every morning. Soybeans and corn crops had replaced the cotton, whose price made it no longer worth planting. The market for cotton had been down for several years. The farmers planted huge fields all around the area, as their incomes depended on two things—the weather and the markets. Such risk plagued the farmer's life.

One of the farmers said he had seen a good number of turkeys over the winter as they wandered around the edges of his fields. Joe appreciated the farmers keeping him posted on the hatch each year.

Joe decided to go home, taking a nap before watching the baseball practice later in the afternoon. With the windows in the house open, the spring breeze flowed through the house as Belle slept at the foot of the bed.

When Joe arrived at the baseball field, the coach had the boys running bases while the infield practiced double plays at second and first. Next, with the bases loaded, they practiced turning double plays at home and first. The session ran long; it was almost six PM before they stopped.

Connor got in the truck, telling Joe what he'd learned.

"Hank Parsons is a senior and first string shortstop, Paw Paw. He's good. He also pitches sometimes. I hope I get to play short in the games when Hank has to pitch."

"That'll be good. Do you think you'll play somewhere else when he's playing short?" Joe asked.

"Probably center, but I don't know how much playing time I'll get this year. Whatever I get, I'll be glad." His demeanor brightened, "So, can we hunt tomorrow?"

"Sure. Let's get home and hook up the boat so we can go to the river. I want to try that bird again."

"I wish we had some more crawdads for catfish bait."

"I've got some frozen shad in the freezer. We'll thaw out some of those. It works pretty well, too," Joe said. "I left the lines in the boat."

"Cool," Connor said.

"Yeah ... cool," Joe said, with a wrinkled smile.

"Paw Paw, you don't sound right when you say it."

"Well, then ... far out."

Connor cackled as Joe laughed, turning into the driveway.

CHAPTER 33 – STIFF KNEES

On Good Friday morning, in the dark, Connor dropped the jars in the creek as Joe guided the boat. The shad, now reduced to small chunks, caused a fishy smell to cling to Connor's fingers. Each time he'd bait a hook, he allowed Joe to inspect it, to make sure he'd done it right before tossing it over the side.

"You gotta hook it two or three times so they can't eat it without taking the hook," Joe said.

Connor was eager to learn. And to show Joe he could do it.

With all the lines in the water, Joe said, "We'll see how well you did when we come back. If all the hooks are bare, we'll know I need a different first mate."

Joe motored close to the high ridge area before securing the boat. They climbed the ridge to dry ground to wait for daylight at the flat place, where Joe had discovered the strut zone on the previous trip.

While standing in the dark, Connor heard something moving along up the hill from where they stood.

In the filtered moonlight under the trees, Connor identified two deer creeping along parallel to the hillside. He watched as they tiptoed past. At one point, Connor detected both deer had no antlers and they were not as big as the buck he'd seen crossing Rocky Hill Road last week.

After the deer passed, Joe said, "Ain't no tellin what you'll see out here."

"They didn't even see us," Connor whispered back.

"If you stay still and they don't catch your scent, they'll never see you. They see movement well. Not as well as a turkey but pretty good. But they can smell you. That's one thing you don't have to worry about with a turkey. If turkeys could smell, I might just give up."

~~~~~~~

Daylight broke, leading Joe to hoot like a barred owl. An owl answered from behind them from across the creek. Other owls chimed in from almost every direction.

A tom gobbled at the hilltop. Just like the other day, he had roosted beside the clear-cut.

"There ain't no use to climb all the way up there. Let's set up here on this flat and wait him out," Joe whispered. "This time, we'll sit facing away from each other 'cause we won't know which way he'll come from ... if he comes. We need to cover all directions. You get on one side of this gum tree with your left side toward the top of the hill. I'll get on the other side."

Joe figured it would be more likely the turkey would come from uphill. Connor, being right handed, could make an easier shot to his left. Joe would take the other side in case the turkey circled around that way.

Joe made two excited cuts followed by a series of yelps. He waited a few seconds before making a cluck. The tom answered from his roost, a hundred yards uphill across the cutover.

With the tom that far away, Joe felt it safe to talk, "He heard the call and he knows it came from his strut zone. I think he'll come eventually unless another hen leads him away again."

~~~~~~~

158

Connor's heart began beating faster as he scanned the area. He found these woods more beautiful than Jones Bluff. The trees on the steep hillside had not been accessible to the loggers; their trunks reached three feet in diameter. Connor had fished with Joe in this area before, but he'd never gotten out of the boat before to explore the woods. He imagined he sat under the same tree where an Indian had sat, back in the old times.

"It might take a long time, so get comfortable but stay alert," Joe said. He saw no need to call again.

The turkey gobbled on his own several more times from the hilltop, then fell silent. Connor tried to stay still while watching the woods closely for any movement. A squirrel climbed a tree nearby, pouncing from one limb to another. A blue jay landed on the ground, collecting something in its beak, before flying away with it. Crows flew overhead, cawing occasionally as they passed from one horizon to the other. Time passed slowly.

Conner reminisced about a conversation he'd had with Joe about time and turkeys. *Time is not a factor in a turkey's life*, Joe had said. *A turkey doesn't have to be anywhere at any certain time. Every minute in their day is like a whole new day, so they don't miss anything. We should all be so lucky as to live like that.*

While he thought about that, he wondered what Janice planned for the day. A scratching sound caught his attention up the hillside to his left. He cut his eyes toward the noise, a smooth round knob that wasn't there before. It resembled an animal, but Connor failed to recognize what kind. After it moved, the smooth knob transformed into the top of a turkey's back. The turkey's head pecked at the ground, out of sight. When the turkey raised its head, Connor could clearly see it as a small hen. Just beyond the hen, stood another. The hens eased along slowly, pecking and scratching the ground. They paused often, raising their heads, scouring the surrounding woods. The hens emitted faint clucks and purrs.

Connor scanned the surrounding area, hoping to see a gobbler.

The group of hens scoured the area for fifteen minutes as Connor and Joe remained frozen. When the hens drifted away far enough for Connor to relax, he straightened out his right leg. His knees had begun to ache from being in the same position so long. As soon as his right leg was flat against the ground, he straightened his left leg out.

The loud flapping of heavy wings exploded in the silence, seventy- five yards uphill. A large turkey had taken to the air, beating his way through trees, heading for the top of the hill. A gobbler, unseen by Connor, had caught sight of Connor's movement.

Connor's heart sank.

Joe peered around the tree toward Connor. "What happened? I never saw that tom until he took off."

Connor thought about lying. He didn't want to disappoint Joe by admitting he had stretched his leg, spooking the turkey. Connor decided to tell the truth, even though it shamed him.

"I moved my leg 'cause my knees ached. I thought the hens had gone. I thought it was safe. I'm sorry, Paw Paw."

Joe rose to his knees, placing his hand against the big tree for support. "Well, you didn't know he was there and neither did I. Some of these ole birds are just blessed with good luck. Don't worry about it. We learned something about this turkey today that we'll use against him next time."

"Dadgummit, Paw Paw. I wish I hadn't moved."

"You know, the best turkeys to hunt are the ones that are hard to kill. I've hunted some for a whole season and never got a shot at them. It's the hunting that really counts anyway. It's not always about the killing."

Connor considered Joe's words as they trudged to the boat. When they eventually got there, he felt better, anxious to recover the lines where he hoped they'd catch some catfish.

After motoring downstream, the first jar danced up and down on the surface before scooting underwater. It quickly popped up a few yards away.

Connor's heart thudded in his chest.

When Joe eased within reaching distance of the jar, it scooted away from the boat. "That's a big one, son. Get the net. Grab the line and pull it gently up until you can get the net under the fish with your other hand," Joe instructed as he handled the tiller.

Each time the boat came close, the jar scooted away before Connor could catch it. On the fifth try, Connor squeezed his hand tight on the jar. The fish surged hard. He leaned forward trying not to rip the hook from the fish's mouth. When the fish came into view, it stretched over two feet long. The fish rolled near the surface, showing a fat, white belly.

Connor slid the net deep in the water before moving it underneath the tired fish. He scooped the fish into the net, releasing the jar, to use both hands on the heavy net's handle. He hauled the fish over the side of the boat, toppling back into the bottom of the boat as the fish flopped between his feet.

"Holy Moley!" Connor yelled.

"Whoo eee! That's a bigun," Joe said as they celebrated their catch. They managed to put the big fish into the livewell. When the fish hit the water inside the well, it flopped violently, causing a loud noise and splashing water. Connor worried it might crack the side of the boat.

The lines produced six more fish, all of them much smaller, but perfect for frying. One of the jars had drifted into the limbs of a large fallen tree. They were unable to get to it, although they observed no indication of a fish on the line.

Heading to the landing, Connor took off his cap, letting the cool air blow through his hair.

I'm Connor McCoy, master angler.

He smiled.

I can't wait to tell Mom ... and Janice.

CHAPTER 34 – SORE MUSCLES

After lunch, Connor received Joe's permission to ride his bike to the Johnson's house. With his baseball glove hanging on the handlebars, he arrived in fifteen minutes. The Johnson boys worked alongside their father on a tractor in the back yard. Connor learned someone had given the old, broken machine to Mr. Johnson. They planned to rebuild it, and try to sell it later.

Janice worked at finishing her Easter dress in the back room. Everyone seemed too busy to visit. Connor offered to help work on the tractor but all he could do was watch as Mr. Johnson took the engine apart.

Mrs. Johnson stepped to the back porch, offering him a glass of iced tea. Connor followed her inside to sit at the kitchen table.

"Janice is almost done," she said. "How's Mr. Joe doing today?"

"He's just fine. We went turkey hunting this morning and caught some catfish."

"At the same time? Well, that must have been tricky."

Connor laughed, "We're pretty tricky."

"Hey." Janice strolled into the kitchen. "What ya' been doing?"

Connor filled her in on the details of the morning's adventure on the river. The three traded stories for an hour as

Mrs. Johnson worked in the kitchen. The casual conversation, filled with friendly banter, eased the nervousness he'd previously felt around her parents.

After an hour passed, Connor said goodbye to Mrs. Johnson before Janice walked him to the front porch to say goodbye.

He pedaled home to spend the rest of the day working with Joe on the farm. They made plans for the next morning's hunt, engaging in long conversations while working together.

Joe had spread a layer of salt on the skin-side of the fox hide. They scraped the wet salt from the hide before layering the fox's skin with a paste made from alum and borax.

Connor tied a rope around the trunk of a tree that had fallen into the back of the field. Joe pulled the log into the woods with the tractor. He watched Joe uncouple the big mower from the tractor before attaching the disk. Connor drove the tractor to disk along the edges of the field. The fresh-tilled dirt's heady scent filled the air. With sunlight fading from the sky, Joe decided to finish the field later.

~~~~~~~

At supper, Connor's aching muscles left him tired but content with the day's work. Helping his grandfather produced a sense of purpose. Connor imagined having a farm of his own someday. These thoughts filled him with satisfaction, knowing a few tired muscles were a small price to pay.

Chapter 35 – The Pitch

The wind had picked up on Saturday's cloudy morning. The Thompson Tract stayed silent as Joe and Connor tried calling from three different locations across the big farm in the early morning, but never heard a turkey.

At one point, Joe told Connor, "This here's a no-gobbling day."

Nancy was to arrive mid-morning. They were excited at the thought of seeing her. Joe decided they should go home to wait for her. With plenty of time for breakfast, Joe prepared fried eggs, grits, and bacon. After eating, Joe and Connor took cups of coffee to the front porch.

Belle barked when Nancy's station wagon turned into the driveway. The dog always barked when company came or anything unusual happened in the yard.

After the customary hugs, they unloaded her luggage. Joe poured a fresh cup for Nancy. Connor talked unceasingly, catching his mother up on the baseball team, the turkey hunting, and things at school.

Since he needed a few minutes alone with Nancy, Joe said, "Connor, I want you to go gather the eggs."

Connor headed to the chicken house with a metal bucket.

Joe planned this to allow enough time to make his pitch to Nancy.

"I found out Pickens Timber Company has a bookkeeping job open. The office is in Monroeville ... you remember Jessie. He's a good man and seems to run a good business. In case you're interested."

"Well, that's only thirty minutes' drive from here. If I got the job, I could buy a house nearby. Do you know what days they work?"

"Monday through Friday. I'm pretty sure of that."

"Give me their number. I'll phone Monday to see if I can get an interview. Let's just keep this to ourselves for now. I don't want Connor getting his hopes up."

"Sounds good." Joe retrieved Jessie Pickens' business card from a kitchen drawer, handing it to her. "Jessie says that Mrs. Baker is who you should talk to. She's in charge of hiring her own replacement."

Joe leaned back in his chair, staring down into his coffee cup.

Things will work out for the best. Good things come to those who wait.

CHAPTER 36 – EASTER SUNDAY

With only time for a short hunt on Easter morning, Joe decided to try Jones Bluff. Joe and Connor stood among the pines on top of the hill as daylight broke.

The gobbler answered Joe's owl-call right away. He roosted just inside the edge of the swamp. They crept down the hill toward him.

A large patch of thick bushes, ten feet wide, lay thirty yards directly in front of where they sat. The turkey gobbled from the other side, about a hundred yards away.

After they settled into position, they relaxed, growing still as if frozen. Joe issued two soft clucks. The tom answered. The sparse pines and hardwoods offered a good view on each side of the thick, tangled, clump of bushes.

After twenty minutes of gobbling with Joe offering a cluck occasionally, the turkey suddenly flew toward them. Instead of landing on the ground, it perched in a small pine sixty yards away, ninety degrees to their left.

By slowly turning his head toward the turkey, Joe spotted him sitting on one of the lower limbs. The bird stretched his neck, searching for the hen that had produced the soft inviting clucks.

Joe sat still, watching the turkey silently surveying the area. He waited on the limb for twenty minutes before spreading his wings to sail to the ground. He landed on the far side of the dense bushes, out of their line of sight.

Joe and Connor eased their cheeks against the stocks of their guns.

Connor pointed his barrel at the right edge of the clump, Joe pointed his to the left edge. Either way the turkey went, one of them would have a good shot.

Joe saw the turkey's head quickly peek out around the bushes, locking its eyes on him. Before he could blink, the turkey pulled its head back behind the brush, immediately sounding the alarm putt. The turkey ran down the hill on the other side of the clump of bushes, out of view, lifting into the air fifty yards away, flying into the swamp.

"Well, I'll be dad blame," Joe said, taking off his hat to slap it against his leg.

Connor's eyes became round, "What happened?"

"He poked his head out and looked right at me. I think he was suspicious anyway. That's why he flew to that pine tree, so he could get a good look around. I guess he just had to get a closer look at us and figured he'd get behind those bushes and peek around."

"Dang, that's a smart turkey."

"You notice how he kept those bushes in between us and him when he ran?"

"He did that on purpose?"

"Oh, yeah … I've seen them do it before. Well, we may as well get on back home."

"Was that the 'durn ole' turkey'?"

"Yep," Joe chuckled, "I believe it was."

~~~~~~

Connor's mother insisted he wear his white shirt with a black tie to church. He didn't like wearing a tie, but he knew he wasted his breath to argue about it. His mama stood her ground on dressing properly for church; he didn't expect her to budge anytime soon.

Janice wore her new yellow dress. Connor noticed her hair looked different. She had pulled it up, exposing more of her face than Connor usually saw.

The dress flowed around her body when she turned. Ruffles enhanced the shoulders. With her hair pulled up, Connor thought she looked older … and even more beautiful. Several of the ladies complimented Janice for her dress.

As she approached, Connor stared at her, "Wow."

That was enough.

Janice, beaming with delight, smiled with a simple, "Hey, you."

A huge crowd filled the sanctuary. Extra folding chairs lined the inside of each pew, even across the open space near the back of the church.

Janice, for the first time, sat with Connor's family during the service. Some of the younger kids eyed them sitting together, whispered and laughed while poking one another. Connor struggled with his embarrassment.

Kids are such a pain.

After church, everyone strolled to the Fellowship Hall for dinner-on-the-ground. Tables inside overflowed with dishes of all types of food brought by the parishioners to share. Connor and Janice sat with her family.

When Joe's family drove home, everyone complained of being full, tired, and sleepy. No one did any work of consequence on Sundays, only tasks that must be done every day, like feeding the chickens, or gathering the eggs.

～～～～～

When Nancy left to drive home, tears trickled down her cheeks for the first two miles. She hated leaving Connor, returning to the solitude of her house. It made her anxious to call Pickens Timber tomorrow to speak to Mrs. Baker about a job interview. Nancy hoped she wasn't too late, finding the job had already been filled.

~~~~~~~

Connor, feeling sad that night, sat with Joe in the living room. Although he liked living with Paw Paw, things *were* different. Even at fourteen, he deeply missed his mother.

Joe rose from his chair, "I'm not feeling too good. I'm going to bed early."

Connor seldom heard his grandfather complain about anything. He noticed Joe's face was pale.

"Do you need anything?" Connor asked.

"No, I'll be okay, probably just overly tired from a busy day. I'll be fine in the morning. You go on to bed soon. I'll see you when you get home tomorrow afternoon."

"Where you hunting in the morning, Paw Paw?"

"I think I'll go back to the Hall Place and see what's going on there. You have a good day at school."

Connor crawled into bed troubled. He wished his mother lived here to make sure Paw Paw was okay. He decided to call her after school tomorrow.

Chapter 37 - Mistake

Joe woke early Monday morning before he drove to The Hall Place to stand on the power line in the dark. The half-moon settled below the horizon as Joe watched it slide away.

The sky lighted as he strolled to the top of a rise overlooking the creek-swamp. A turkey gobbled far to the right of the power line. Joe weaved through the trees toward the sound.

When he'd traveled half the distance, a turkey flew from a tree above his head. Then several others flew from their roosts nearby. Joe watched six hens vacate the area.

He kept moving toward the gobbler until he estimated being close enough. He sat, leaning his back against a tree. When he made the first call, the turkey gobbled from the thick canopy, directly above his head.

The leaves on the trees had grown full, having made the gobbler sound farther away. The thickening foliage had buffered the sound waves. Joe knew he had made a mistake.

He sat studying the limbs of the trees above his head, trying to detect a turkey in the dim light. He couldn't call again for fear the tom might see his movement.

All I can do is sit here and hope he flies down in front of me.

He waited ten minutes before the turkey gobbled again. Still, he failed to spot the turkey in the thick canopy. A few minutes later, a limb cracked as the big turkey pushed off. His wings beat the air. Joe watched the tom fly toward the power line.

Joe maneuvered within fifty yards of the power line to observe the open ground through the trees. The tom answered every call he sent for the next hour, but refused to leave the safety of the power line. Twice, Joe caught a glimpse of the tom moving back and forth beyond the bushes.

Eventually, a hen joined the gobbler. The gobbler grew silent and left the area, following the hen. Joe went home regretting his mistake in moving too close to the gobbler but happy to have another story to tell.

~~~~~~~

Nancy's morning break time at ten AM allowed her to hurry down the street to a pay phone, where she dropped in a handful of dimes before dialing long-distance for Pickens Timber.

Mrs. Baker answered the phone. Nancy, not sure if she liked the idea of a job where she would answer the phone as well as being the bookkeeper, introduced herself.

She discovered, to her surprise, that Mrs. Baker was expecting her call.

"Jessie told me you'd be calling," Mrs. Baker said, "I've known your daddy for a long time. You just tell me when you can come up here, sweetie. We'll make plans to talk with you."

Nancy set the appointment for Wednesday morning. She would have to take another vacation day to drive to Uriah Tuesday night. She hated driving that far in the dark, but she was anxious to learn what the job entailed.

She wondered how her daddy sent the word to Jessie so soon. Then it dawned on her that Daddy had spoken to Jessie before he told her about the job. The revelation amused her.

That stinker.

~~~~~~~

When Connor came home from school, Joe napped in his chair. Belle greeted Connor at the door, which woke Joe. Connor worked on his homework at the kitchen table. Joe went to the barn. At five thirty, the phone rang.

"Hello, Joe's residence," Connor said.

"Hey, Connor, it's Mama," Nancy said.

"Hey, Mama, I was gonna call you in just a little while."

"Oh. What about?"

"Paw Paw was feeling bad last night and he didn't look so good. I just wanted you to know."

"Is he okay today?"

"Yes, ma'am, I think so. He went hunting this morning, so I guess he feels better. He's in the barn working on something."

"Good. Keep an eye on him for me. He doesn't let anybody know when he's hurt or sick if he can help it. And he won't go to the doctor unless you push him. Paw Paw will be sixty-eight in May so we need to be sure he's taking care of himself. You've got to watch him, okay?" she said. "Listen, I'm coming to Uriah tomorrow night. I'll check on him then."

"Why are you coming tomorrow night?"

Nancy had not fully prepared for telling Connor she considered changing jobs this soon. She didn't want him to get his hopes high in case she didn't get the job.

"Oh, there's a job for a bookkeeper in Monroeville. I thought I'd check it out. I have an interview but, you know, it's probably nothing."

"Wow. I didn't know you would consider a job up there."

"I'm just mostly curious. You never know."

"That would be so cool."

"It's just an interview."

"Well, okay, I'll see you tomorrow night."

"Okay, bye Connor … love you."

"I love you too, Mama."

Later, Connor told Joe about the call.

Joe put his hands on his hips, "Well, maybe she can get a job up here. Wouldn't that be something? But don't count your chickens before they hatch, boy."

"Yes, sir, I won't. How'd the hunt go this morning?"

"I messed up right off the bat." Joe laughed. "I ended up walkin' right under a bunch of hens and scaring them all off and then, to top things off, I sat down under the gobbler. I couldn't move a muscle. Couldn't even pull my call out of my vest. He eventually flew out ... went to the power line and strutted 'till a hen led him off."

Connor laughed.

If Paw Paw can make a mistake, I don't feel so bad about my own.

"I brought home a book from the school library about Auburn's programs. Maybe we could learn more about the forestry and wildlife programs there."

"Let's sit down and have a look, son."

They spent the rest of the evening talking about college.

As Connor lay in bed that night, he wondered about his mom's job interview.

What will happen if Mama decides to move?

The possibility excited him.

CHAPTER 38 – BEST MEDICINE

Joe skipped hunting on Tuesday morning. When he woke at the usual time that morning, he felt unusual. He rose from the bed, becoming disoriented. His dizziness caused him to sit down on the bed again. Unusually tired, he decided to stay in to rest.

After an hour of rest, he rose to prepare Connor's breakfast before seeing him off to school. Afterward, he climbed in the truck to drive to Atmore. He arrived at Dr. Stewart's office at nine fifteen.

The doctor examined Joe, probing him with many questions. Writing on a note pad, the doctor said, "Joe, I'm going to set an appointment over at the hospital as soon as possible. They stay pretty booked-up over there. I want you to have some tests done. That's the only way to know what's going on for sure."

"Alright, Doc, that'll be fine."

"Meanwhile, have this prescription filled on the way home. It will help with your symptoms until we figure this thing out." He handed Joe the piece of paper.

Joe drove to the drug store to buy the medicine. As soon as he returned home, the phone rang. The lady at the doctor's office explained it would be three weeks from today before they had an opening for the appointment. April twenty-ninth. Joe noted the day and time on the calendar in the kitchen, glad it would be after turkey season.

He picked up Connor after baseball practice. They spent the rest of the day working on the home place. Connor had most of the field disked by sunset. Joe planned to plant corn in the field soon. He had mentioned he might buy a couple of pigs to fatten them up on the corn until winter when they would butcher them. They planned to upgrade the old hog pen before summer, keeping the pigs in a reinforced pen.

~~~~~~

Connor was happy to think of summer vacation on Joe's farm. Growing corn, raising two pigs, while spending time with Paw Paw. He looked forward to Janice's birthday, which would come this weekend, and what they could do this summer.

When his mother arrived, they had supper on the table waiting for her. As they settled in to eat, Connor questioned her about the job interview. After Connor listened all the details, they'd finished supper. Nancy insisted that she do the dishes, allowing Connor and Joe to rest on the front porch.

When Nancy finished the dishes, she joined them.

Connor folded his arms across his chest, "Mama, do you think it's okay to go steady at my age?"

Nancy raised an eyebrow, "Are you thinking of asking Janice?"

"Yes, ma'am. I'm thinking about it."

"I suppose. She's turning fourteen and you'll be fifteen in October." Nancy grinned, "You know, when Paw Paw was young, people got married at fourteen."

Surprised, Connor's eyes widened, "Really? Good grief."

Nancy turned to her father, "Daddy, Connor said you were feeling bad Sunday night?"

"Yeah, but I'm okay now. I think I just overdid it that day. My brain keeps trying to convince my body that we're still in our twenties," Joe said.

"Well, you'll let me know if anything's wrong, won't you?" Nancy said.

"I reckon."

Connor returned to the more interesting subject, "Paw Paw, how old were you when you got married?"

"Why? You thinking we might need a preacher soon?"

"Heck, no!" Connor yelled.

Joe laughed, "I reckon I was around twenty or so. I had to get married to save money."

"What do you mean, Paw Paw?"

"I was spending all my money driving back and forth to her mama's house."

The laughter was good medicine. They sat, enjoying the cool spring night on the front porch. The whip-o-wills called to one another in the dark woods.

CHAPTER 39 – DURN OLE TURKEY

The next morning Joe drove to Jones Bluff. This ole turkey had gotten under his skin. Joe couldn't let it rest. The pills the doctor had prescribed seemed to help. Joe's old energy returned.

Joe descended halfway along the hill before daylight broke. He owled. A tom gobbled. This time, the ole bird roosted deep in the swamp. Joe hiked toward the distant sound. When he stepped inside the edge of the bottomland, he paused to owl again. He remembered the leaves on the trees made turkey gobbles sound farther away. He wanted to hear the tom gobble again to be sure he hadn't wandered too close.

The turkey gobbled two hundred yards in front of Joe. A canopy of trees sheltered the creek bottom, providing dappled shade. Joe worried if he came much closer he risked being seen. A nagging thought worried Joe.

This ole bird has been called several times from this direction, spooking him at least once or twice. If I call him from here, he'll be mighty suspicious.

Joe wheeled around and trekked along the edge of the creek bottom to scoot along parallel to it for two hundred yards. He reentered the bottom, sneaking for another hundred yards directly into the flats. Joe had gotten parallel to the gobbler, at the same level as the bird, deep in the creek bottom. The creek bottom spread wide from years of spring floods.

Even though he had slinked a hundred yards deep into it, he still hadn't reached the creek.

Joe sat, reclining back against a big red oak tree, before pulling the box call from his vest. He made three soft yelps before easing the call onto the ground. The shotgun rested on his left knee.

The turkey responded one time. Joe lingered. Thirty minutes passed with no turkey sounds or wind noise. The woods were so quiet Joe felt sure he could hear the gobbler if he swooped to the ground.

Another fifteen minutes passed, but Joe did not call again. Then, the sound of wings made a faint, *swoosh, swoosh.*

Joe visually probed among the ferns and fallen logs toward the sound's origin for any sign of the bird. Ten minutes passed. Joe determined he'd win, vowing to out-wait the gobbler by staying still, hidden well behind two ferns in front of him. His head, forming the only thing that remained exposed above the understory, rested against the tree's dark trunk.

At the two o'clock position, forty yards in front of him, he caught a movement. The tom's head raised above the ferns like the periscope of an enemy submarine. Joe's eyes froze on the turkey, squinting his eyes almost shut, afraid he would see them.

Eventually, the turkey eased a few steps forward while lowering his head behind the ferns. Joe slid the gun to a position ahead of the tom's path. When the tom's head rose again to check his surroundings, it was several yards from where it had been before. Joe didn't budge. His gun was pointed slightly ahead of the tom. The big bird took a few more steps before dipping his head out of sight again. Joe laid his cheek against the stock.

The next time the big gobbler's head was in view, it paused at thirty yards, straight past the business end of the shotgun. Joe slid the barrel a quarter of an inch right as the bead covered the tom's bright red and blue head. Joe pulled the trigger.

The ole turkey bounced backward, flapping its wings as if airborne. His powerful legs propelled him backwards for ten yards before the flopping ceased. When Joe raced to the bird lying on its side, its legs were moving in slow motion back and forth while its wings slowly raised, paused and returned to his sides.

Joe knelt in the wet ground beside the bird, experiencing a wide range of emotions. Excitement like a child, sadness the hunt had ended, and respect for the critter who had outsmarted him on several occasions.

A sharp pain speared Joe's upper back. He'd never had such a pain before. His left arm lost feeling, growing numb. He laid the gun on the ground. He put both hands on his knees, leaning forward with his head lowered until the feeling passed, before he caught his breath.

Joe took his time carrying his prize up the hill toward the truck. He stopped several times to catch his breath. He needed to get home to take a rest. The lingering ache was still tensing his upper back.

After returning home, he cleaned the bird in the barn. Joe went inside and poured a tall glass of ice water before sitting in his chair. The breeze through the open windows refreshed him. Joe slept there until lunch.

CHAPTER 40 – THE INTERVIEW

Nancy arrived at Pickens Timber Company's office at nine forty-five. The simple wooden building had four rooms along with a restroom. Mrs. Baker's office sat to the right of the lobby.

In the lobby, two stuffed deer heads hung on the cedar-planked walls. On one wall hung framed, faded photographs of logging operations, new trucks, and colored men, standing beside huge piles of logs. Nancy noticed one photo of two men standing on the porch of a large house. The photo showed Jessie Pickens beside her daddy. The men were much younger.

When Nancy came into Mrs. Baker's office, she noticed a dozen file cabinets lined the walls. She rose from her chair to greet Nancy. Short and round, Mrs. Baker wore a beautiful head of silver hair.

They talked for almost two hours. However, it wasn't all business. Mrs. Baker and Nancy discovered they had dozens of mutual acquaintances while discussing families they knew.

Mrs. Baker listened close as Nancy described her experience in reconciling ledgers and bank accounts, calculating payroll and preparing monthly income/expense statements.

After Nancy described the details of her experience in bookkeeping, she asked several questions about the business.

Eventually, Mrs. Baker said, "One last question dear, do you prepare taxes?"

"Of course," Nancy replied.

"You're a godsend. How soon can you start?"

The amount of cash flow impressed Nancy. As did the salary they offered. Nancy accepted the job.

They agreed to begin work on a Monday, April twenty-first, in just twelve days. Mrs. Baker planned to stay as long as needed to complete Nancy's training before retiring.

Pickens Lumber paid their employees by check every Friday. Mrs. Baker warned Nancy, "Fridays are very busy. The company runs twenty-two log trucks, and we have over forty-five employees. All the drivers, saw-hands, and cruisers come to the office to collect their pay. You'll get to know them all."

Nancy bubbled with excitement on the drive to Uriah. It had been a long time since life events made her this happy. Over and over in her mind, she planned on how to tell Connor and Joe. She pondered how to go about selling the house in Mobile while pursuing a place of her own in Uriah or Monroeville.

She considered her friends at church in Mobile, too.

How will I break the news to them? So much to do. So much to plan for.

She turned on the radio, tapping her fingers against the steering wheel, keeping time while singing along with The Archies,' "Sugar-Sugar."

When Nancy pulled into Joe's driveway, he was sitting on the front steps chopping at Belle's hair with a big pair of scissors.

"Daddy, you're getting dog hair all over the steps."

"I'll sweep it off when I'm through. Here, hold her collar for me so I can get these cockleburs out of her tail. She traipsed off somewhere and came back full of them."

Nancy gripped the collar while stroking Belle's head.

"How'd it go with the interview?" Joe said.

Teasing, she said, "Well ... I don't know ... you think you could put up with me for a while until I can find a place to live?"

"What? You mean you took the job already?" Joe laughed.

"I start Monday after next."

"Well, I'll be." Joe couldn't mask his excitement. He grinned while slapping his knee. "Connor's gonna be so happy."

"I am too, Daddy. I am too."

Belle sensed their excitement, creating a playful growl before lurching upward to lick Nancy on the mouth.

Nancy squealed, spit, wiped her mouth, and laughed.

When Connor leaped off the bus, he ran to the front porch where Joe and Nancy waited. Both stared down into their coffee cups, not saying a word.

Noticing the way their heads were bowed, Connor whispered, "What happened?"

"What do you mean?" Nancy said.

"About the job, Mama."

Nancy gazed at her son. All her plans for keeping cool, playing a little trick on Connor went south. "I got the job!" she screamed.

Connor jumped high in the air, landing before hugging his mother. Nancy and Connor planned and dreamed for the rest of the afternoon about what kind of house they wanted to buy and discussed what this meant to their futures.

Joe spent the afternoon on the tractor, getting the field ready to plant corn. When the time arrived for Nancy to go, Joe hugged her for a longer time than usual before whispering, "I'm so glad you're coming home."

Nancy drove to Mobile with tears again, but this time—happy tears.

~~~~~~

That night at supper, Joe found time to tell Connor about the turkey he'd killed that morning, "Well, I reckon that 'durn ol' turkey' is now a 'dead ol' turkey.'"

Connor put the spurs and beard Joe showed him in the Mason jar along with the others, happy for his grandpa outwitting the smart ole gobbler.

CHAPTER 41 – BUBBLING CRUDE

The following afternoon, during baseball practice, Connor learned the first game would take place Saturday, one week and two days away. He had been moving between shortstop, third base and center field in most of the practices.

He also pitched for a while during one batting practice. Connor had settled in comfortably with the team as well as the school. Word had spread that he and Janice were an item since they spent most of the break times together. Connor knew a few boys in school were jealous. Positive that Janice had been sought after before, he tried to ignore the boys who tried to flirt with her. He knew Janice could handle any advances she may encounter. Still, he felt protective.

~~~~~~

Joe had hunted the morning at the Thompson Track but failed to bring a turkey close. After returning home, he stayed busy the rest of the day planting corn.

In the slow "granny" gear, the tractor pulled a one-row planter, opening a furrow, dropping a seed every five or six inches, covering them with two inches of dirt as it went. Joe worked to guide the tractor's front wheel, following the straight rows while keeping an eye on the planter behind, in case it clogged.

After he finished planting, Joe applied two dozen sacks of fertilizer, to ensure the corn would grow tall and produce good ears. Working alone made the process slow and tedious.

185

~~~~~~~

After Connor finished homework, he and Joe checked the hog pen to plan the needed repairs. The pen sat to the right of the field, stowed away in the woods. Joe didn't require a big pen, one only about twenty yards square. Some years ago, Joe had split a fifty-five-gallon metal drum in half from top to bottom. The two sides served as a feed trough and a water trough. Metal stakes had been driven into the ground around them to prevent the pigs from pushing the troughs, spilling the contents. The ground inside the pen contained a half-dozen one-foot-deep holes caused by the previous hogs wallowing in the mud. Weeds lined the fence, with a few places along the fence needing repair. Joe explained to Connor that the most important part of the fence is buried in the ground to keep the hogs from rooting under it to get out.

"I figure we'll buy two shoats in June. So, we have some time to patch up this old pen. We'll feed 'em whatever we can that's low in price until the corn dries in the field around August. Hopefully, the coons and deer won't eat too much of the field corn. We'll use the corn to finish fattening them up. Corn-fed pork is better tasting," Joe said.

"What else do pigs eat?"

"Pigs will eat just about anything. Scraps from the garden and the kitchen are their favorite but we'll buy a few sacks of feed, too.

"When do we butcher them?"

"We'll catch a real cold morning for butchering. You need it cold. Less chance of the meat spoiling and less flies to deal with."

"So, after we kill them, we'll just skin them out?"

"You'll see how all that's done. We don't skin hogs like we did the deer you killed last fall. We scrape the hair off.

You'll see. There's nothing better than fresh fried pork with some syrup and biscuits."

"How do you scrape the hair off? Seems like that would take a long time and be hard to do."

"Well, you have to boil water in that black pot first," Joe pointed at a big cast iron pot with three short legs on the bottom. The black pot sat under a nearby tree. "You build a fire under that pot of water then you pour the hot water in a barrel that's sort of lying on its side in a hole that you dig. You take the hog and dip him in the hot water, that makes the hair turn loose of the hide and it scrapes right off, clean as a baby's butt."

"Oh."

"You can dip the hot water out and pour it on the hog, too. It's better to show you than to try to explain it. You'll see."

Then Connor recalled the birthday party, "Paw Paw, Janice's birthday is Saturday. Can I go to her house and have cake around three o'clock?"

"Sure, you wouldn't want to miss that."

On the way to the house, they stopped at the chicken pen, shutting the gate before going in for supper.

~~~~~~

The next morning, Joe drove back to the Thompson Tract. He heard the two toms gobble during the morning. He planned to have Connor there the next morning. Joe didn't want to mess with them until then. He wanted Connor to call on his own tomorrow again.

That afternoon, Joe had a visitor soon after Connor arrived from school. A white and red Rambler drove in the driveway just before dark. The man got out, glancing about before stepping to the porch.

"Howdy, Mr. Parker?" he asked.

"That's right," Joe shook the man's hand.

"I'm Charles Drew. I work for the Red Clay Oil Company. My company wants to buy the mineral rights on your land. Red Clay is planning to test for oil in Monroe County and we're offering to buy mineral rights from landowners across the county. I have an offer here. Take this and call that number with any questions."

He handed Joe a folder with a logo printed on the front.

"Most all the information's in there," he said.

Joe said, "I'll consider the offer and let you know."

The man handed Joe a card. They shook hands as they said goodbye.

Inside the house, Joe said, "I never heard of any oil around these parts. Sounds like I'll have to talk to some neighbors about this. I bet Jessie will know something about it."

"Maybe they'll strike oil and we'll all be rich! Like the Beverly Hillbillies," Connor said laughing.

"Be careful what you wish for, son. If they strike oil, you can kiss all these woods goodbye. It'll end the turkey hunting, too. Speaking of turkey hunting, get my box and practice your calling a while. You're gonna be on your own again tomorrow."

Connor retrieved the call from Joe's vest, applying some fresh chalk before sitting on the porch swing to practice while Joe cleaned the kitchen. Joe joined him on the front porch swing later to give him some pointers.

"Your mom will be here early tomorrow, but I told her we'd be back around ten," Joe said. "She's gonna have a lot of stuff to unload, I reckon. She's getting a head start on the move."

"Good. Just one more week before she'll be here all the time," Connor said.

"Yep, it sure is going to be nice having a house full again," Joe said. "Here, let me show you how to make a fly-down cackle call."

Connor handed the call to Joe while he marveled at Joe's technique, like listening to someone play a fine-tuned musical instrument.

CHAPTER 42 – STEADY

Fog lay heavy heading to the Thompson Tract. It slowed the drive to their hunt, forcing Joe to use the windshield wipers.

After parking the truck, they hiked across the big pasture in the dark, soaking their pants legs from the dew on the tall grass before they reached the woods beyond.

No toms gobbled in the fog while they listened. Between the heavy fog and the foliage of the trees, it would be hard for the sound to carry any distance.

Connor made several calls during the early light with no response. They listened from several places during the morning before settling on a plan to sit in a place to watch the pasture from a rise in the land.

After the fog burned away, letting the sun shine on the big pasture, they sat together, talking while watching the green pasture below.

"Paw Paw, Daddy didn't like to hunt much, did he?" Connor said.

"He went with me a few times but no, he didn't have hunting in his blood, son."

"He liked sports, especially baseball."

"Yes, he did. He was good at it, too," Joe said, giving the boy plenty of time to keep talking.

"I was so mad when he died."

"We were all real sad," Joe said. "Sometimes, life gives us hard things to deal with."

"Paw Paw, things will get better, won't they?"

"They will. Time will heal most wounds. But you'll always miss your daddy. I still miss mine after all these years, son. Life changes. It won't ever stay the same."

"Did your daddy hunt?"

"Not much. He taught me how to kill squirrels and rabbits … those sure came in handy during the Depression."

"I'm glad I came to live with you."

"Me, too, Connor. I like having you with me."

Joe spotted something in the edge of the pasture, pointing to let Connor watch. A bobcat trotted along the edge. They watched until it went out of sight into the woods at the far end. A group of crows landed in the middle of the pasture, hopping around while pecking at the ground. Connor leaned back, drifting off to sleep. Joe listened to his steady breathing, letting him be.

When they arrived home, Nancy had unloaded the station wagon. She arranged her bedroom, hanging her clothes in the closet before stuffing the chest of drawers.

Joe cooked fried-egg-and-bacon sandwiches for a midmorning meal before he drove to the feed store for supplies. Nancy and Connor cleaned house before wrapping Janice's birthday present. The time came for Connor to go, pedaling to Janice's birthday party.

~~~~~~~

When Connor parked his bicycle in the Johnson's front yard, several cars had already parked there. A few parents of Janice's friends stayed for the party. As the house filled, everyone sang happy birthday, gathering around a large white birthday cake with fourteen candles.

Janice pulled her hair back, leaning over to blow out the candles before her mother served everyone cake.

Janice and Connor took their cake outside to sit on the front porch swing. Nobody joined them. Connor knew he had an opportunity. He reached in his pocket, pulling out the small wrapped package before handing it to her, "Happy birthday."

Janice opened the package, smiling as she peeked at the silver necklace with the cross.

Connor whispered, "Will you go steady with me?"

Janice gripped the package with both hands, clenching it to her chest. "Yes, I wondered if you'd ever ask."

Connor wanted to kiss Janice again but the window into the living room sat right behind the swing. He knew someone would see them. He reached across to take her hand, squeezing it, concealing her hand from the view of anyone inside.

He helped Janice put the necklace on before they went inside where she opened other presents.

When Connor returned home, Joe had the hood of the truck open while he lay under the truck. He had drained the oil, screwing the plug back into the pan on the engine. After asking Joe what he could do to help, Connor poured the new oil into the hole at the top of the engine while Joe removed a shallow bucket filled with black, burnt oil from under the truck.

"Take care of what you have and you won't have to buy new things all the time," Joe said. "If you want your things to last a long time, a little bit of effort maintaining equipment will save you lots of work and money."

Connor poured the last quart of oil in the engine while he listened.

"Try not to waste anything. We'll save that burnt oil. It may come in handy later."

"What can you use that for, Paw Paw?"

"Some folks use it with sulfur, to treat mange on dogs. I mostly wipe it on my farm equipment to prevent rust and loosen joints. You can also paint it on wooden posts, to help prevent rot."

It always amazed Connor how much old equipment Joe kept in the barn. Paw Paw maintained it all to keep everything in good shape.

"Let's go after the river bird next Saturday. We only have two more weeks of season left. I want to try something new on that bird before it's over," Joe said. "We'll put out some more lines, too. I gave the last catch to Aubrey and Velma."

Connor wondered when he had taken the fish to the Johnsons. "I would love to see that ol' river bird again," Connor said. "I messed up last time. I want one more chance."

Joe cocked his head to the sky, "It's gonna rain tonight so we might not get to hunt before church tomorrow."

"Okay, maybe if it quits tomorrow afternoon, we could go for an afternoon scout?"

"Sounds good to me. Let's see what the weather does."

"Do you think my beard and spurs have dried yet? I'd like to put them on a piece of wood and hang them in my room,"

"Let's do that right now," Joe said.

They spent the afternoon attaching the beard and spurs to an old grey plank of wood. Joe attached some wire to the back with small nails. Connor hung it in his bedroom beside a set of six-point antlers that came from the first deer Connor ever killed, back in the fall. Another turkey beard with spurs hung on the wall from his first gobbler he'd killed, two springs ago.

Joe pulled the other beards from the Mason jar, wrapping them in freezer paper before he opened the lid of the big freezer in the back room. As Connor watched, Joe carefully removed a cardboard box. The faded red letters on the outside of the waxed box read *Fresh Catfish*.

He lifted the lid revealing the box almost full of turkey beards and spurs.

Connor asked how many were in there.

Joe said he'd never counted them. He placed his new beards in the box and shut the lid, returning the box to the freezer.

"This is just a way to remember the birds, I reckon. But Connor, the most important way to respect the wild turkey is the way you hunt them. You never shoot one in a tree or running in front of dogs. If you do that, you can't be proud of it because you didn't call it to you.

"Call the turkey to you. Do it the right way. Have respect. Just the way you would do things out of respect to remember your daddy. You want to live in a way that'd make him proud."

Connor considered what Joe said. "I understand."

"Good. Let's go get some supper. I think we're having fried turkey breast again," Joe said.

~~~~~~

They entered the kitchen where Nancy set the table.

"She liked the necklace, Mama," Connor said.

"Oh, good. I'm glad she did," Nancy replied.

Connor nudged closer to his mom who stood at the kitchen sink. Joe washed his hands in the bathroom.

"We're going steady," he whispered. Nancy put her arm around his shoulder, giving him a hug.

CHAPTER 43 —ANTICIPATION

Sunday morning brought thunder and lightning. The electricity in the house had gone out sometime during the night. When they arrived at church, the storm had moved away. Connor, happy to see Janice wearing the necklace, asked her to sit with his family. With her parents' permission, she joined them on the pew.

Back home after lunch, Joe and Connor drove to the Thompson Tract to scout the roads and fields for fresh tracks. They watched a group of hens in the rear of one of the fields. They were happy to see a few gobbler tracks on the roads.

The week passed without anything unusual. The corn had sprouted, reaching two inches tall. The week's rain had eased Joe's concern for the corn crop. He hunted every morning but did not shoot a turkey.

Joe cut six new fence posts from small oaks around the property to repair the fence around the hog pen while Connor attended to school and baseball practice.

The coach told the team Hank Parsons would pitch in Saturday's opening game, meaning Connor would play shortstop. The schedule called for a night game, allowing Connor time to rest after the morning hunt.

His mother worked her last week at her old job, making tensions high after she had given her official notice the week before. She could hardly wait until Friday night when she could pack the car with the last of her clothes, makeup, and jewelry for the trip to Uriah Saturday morning. She had contacted a real estate agent who already advertised her house for sale.

Turkey season would end Friday, April twenty-fifth. Connor knew his last opportunity to kill a turkey came this weekend.

Janice visited Connor at Joe's house after school on Wednesday. They spent most of the time on the front porch swing with tall glasses of lemonade, talking. Sneaking kisses while handholding had become common, much to Connor's delight.

Janice planned to attend the game by riding on the bus with other students on Saturday night for the trip to Monroeville. The team traveled on a separate bus. She liked baseball and loved to see her brother play. She was excited at the thought of watching Connor play for the first time.

Kenny batted clean-up in the fourth spot as the power hitter. It thrilled her whenever he knocked one over the fence.

Connor's excitement peaked on Friday afternoon. The big weekend had arrived. Connor and Joe prepared the boat for the next morning's hunt at the river.

CHAPTER 44 – THE RIVER BIRD

After dropping the lines in the creek, they secured the boat to the bank. Joe and Connor climbed to the strut zone, halfway up the hill. Sure enough, the ole tom gobbled from the hilltop cutover.

Before Connor squatted to sit, Joe said, "Wait, I want you to call once, then we'll go halfway to him."

Connor grasped the cedar box, cupping it in his left hand. With his right hand, he slid the lid over the box, producing a series of yelps. After the tom answered, they trudged up the hill toward the top.

Joe gasped for breath when they reached the halfway point, locating a good place to set up. They pruned a few bushes to stick in front of them, settling in to wait. Their field of vision ranged up the hill through the underbrush to the edge of the cutover as it opened to treeless ground.

After waiting thirty minutes, Connor spotted the gobbler silhouetted against the morning sky at the top of the hill, "I see him," he whispered.

The big black bird paraded into the edge of the woods, pausing often to strut and drum. Connor felt the vibrato in his chest.

The tom dawdled for thirty minutes until, finally, it stood within thirty yards of Connor's gun. The tom was close enough to kill but his head and neck lay blocked behind a tree from Connor's line of sight. Joe had a clear shot from his position, but did not pull the trigger. After what seemed like minutes, the turkey took a step forward. Connor placed the sight's bead on its neck halfway from his head to his shoulders before pulling the trigger.

The big gobbler flopped and rolled down the steep hill toward them, stopping only ten yards in front of Connor who sprang to his feet, trotting to the dead bird.

He glanced toward Joe, raised his gun over his head, whooping like an Indian while stepping toward the bird.

Joe rose slowly, using the tree for support before straightening his knees. He limped to the turkey as Connor knelt beside the still bird.

Joe knelt, too, admiring the spurs, "Boy, that's a five-year-old gobbler. You won't kill a lot of these."

The years had allowed the spurs to grow well over an inch long, curving to needle-sharp points.

"See, when you hunt them the right way and you're finally successful, it means a lot more," Joe said.

"We did it the right way, Paw Paw," Connor said resting his hand on Joe's shoulder.

"Yep, we did. And I hope you'll always do that, in whatever you do," Joe said. "I won't always be here to see it happen, but I'll be with you."

Connor jerked his head around in surprise to stare at Joe, his eyes wide and mouth agape, not knowing what to say. He realized his Paw Paw had grown old but the thought of losing him refused to register in his young mind until that moment.

After a moment, Connor quietly answered, "Yes, sir, I know."

They descended the hill to the creek, loading into the boat before motoring along the creek to check the lines. Most of the jars bobbed against the surface of the creek. They only caught two catfish. Upon lifting one line, Connor discovered the hook held a live snake. He quickly let go, letting it slip back in the water. Joe retrieved his shotgun, loading one shell in the right barrel before sliding over near the side of the boat.

"Put that paddle under the jar and swipe the line across the water. When the snake comes to the surface, I'll shoot him," Joe said.

Connor shoved the paddle blade against the side of the line, sweeping it hard to the right. The snake rose close enough to the surface for Joe to see it before he shot. Water exploded with the blast, showering them as the snake floated to the surface. Connor raised the jar into the boat after cutting the line, ditching the dark-colored cottonmouth moccasin in the water.

When they idled near the landing, John Hudson, the catfish man sat on the bait store's porch. He waddled over to meet them as they loaded the boat onto the trailer. Connor showed Mr. Hudson the big turkey while Joe thanked him for telling him where the turkey had gobbled earlier in the season.

They drove toward the café. Connor knew he had plenty of time to clean the bird before resting for his first game tonight. On the way, he contemplated what life would be like if his grandfather passed away and vowed to make the most of the time he had with him.

At the café, Glen Pace with two other local farmers chatted while drinking coffee. When Joe walked in, he said, "I want y'all to come out here and see one of the best turkeys I have ever seen in my life."

They carried their coffee cups to the back of the truck, admiring the big turkey. When told that Connor had killed it, they slapped him on the back with congratulatory praise.

Connor's eyes shone large and bright while Joe bragged on him. During their meal, people would come in, hear about the bird, go out to the truck to take a gander at the big gobbler, then come back in to congratulate him.

On the way home, Connor said, "Can I take some of the meat to Janice's family today?"

"I think that would be a good thing," Joe said.

After they cleaned the turkey, Connor wrapped one side of the big breast in waxed paper before placing it in a grocery sack. Joe drove to the Johnsons' house. Janice was away. Connor gave the sack to Mrs. Johnson at the front porch, briefly explaining the hunt. He jogged back to the truck to return home.

Exhausted, Connor lay in his bed, sleeping for two hours.

CHAPTER 45 - THE GAME

Shouts and laughter shook the team's bus as it departed a full hour before the student bus would leave. The boys wore their team uniforms. The coach drove the bus. They opened the windows until the late afternoon air grew chilly. After they arrived at Monroe High School, they unloaded the gear before going to the visitor's dugout.

After warm-up exercises and fielding, people began to arrive. Monroe High was a big school. Its athletic teams were always in high contention for the regional championship title. Everyone wanted to see each team's first game to determine how they matched up. As the crowd began to grow, Connor spotted Janice in the crowd, sitting with Joe and Nancy, who had driven there to see the game.

Connor noticed Jessie Pickens sat beside Joe. The big man wore overalls with a red flannel shirt.

The first four innings were scoreless. Connor had fielded three ground balls, turning one double play plus two outs thrown to first. The team worked well together. Team spirit was obvious, with lots of yelling and encouragement among teammates.

In the bottom of the fifth, Monroe scored two runs with a single, a triple followed by a sacrifice fly, allowing the runner on third base to tag before beating the throw home.

In the top of the seventh, Uriah tied the game with a walk, then a home run hit by Kenny. Monroe came back with a vengeance.

With one out, the bases were loaded. The coach called time-out, walking to the mound. Hank Parsons assured the coach his arm felt good—he could finish pitching the game. The coach left him in.

The next batter slammed a shot between third and short. Connor backhanded the ball in the hole, flipping it to the third baseman, who waited on the bag. The third baseman threw to first, beating the runner by inches, leaving the game tied.

Connor had walked, flied out and hit one single so far. He batted first in the next inning, slashing a line drive down the third base line, then beat the throw to second base. The next batter struck out. Kenny Johnson came to bat. He cracked a high fly ball to the center field fence, but the ball didn't quite make it over. The fielder caught the fly. Connor tagged, speeding to third. As he turned third base, the ball had just reached the shortstop, who'd made the cut-off beyond second base. Connor dug in, heading for home. He slid into the plate just under the tag; his knee connected with the catcher's cleats as the two tumbled in the red dirt. Safe! Blacksher moved one run ahead. The next batter struck out, ending the inning.

When Monroe came to bat at the bottom of the last inning, they had the top of their line-up scheduled to bat. Hank struck out the first batter. The second batter drilled a hot grounder at Connor. Connor fired a shot to first for the second out. The third batter hit a long fly ball, but the right-fielder caught it at the fence to end the game.

The team had won their first game of the year, celebrating all the way to Uriah with the buses honking their horns along the dark county roads.

The excitement, the game, and the celebration left Connor exhausted. After bandaging his cut knee-cap, he decided not to go turkey hunting the next morning, so Joe decided to stay home, too.

The next morning, at church, the Baptist preacher congratulated the team before the sermon. Connor invited Janice to have Sunday dinner at his house. After dinner, Connor walked her home along the long dirt road.

Chapter 46 – Forever

At eight AM Monday morning, Nancy began her first day of work for Pickens Timber. The office stayed busy. Mrs. Baker proved to be a good teacher, explaining how the business worked. She gave Nancy a schedule of things to do, along with when they needed to be done each month.

Nancy knocked off work at five, driving to Uriah. The thirty-minute drive allowed her to arrive at home with plenty of daylight remaining. She had insisted that she prepare supper every night. In turn, Joe insisted on doing the dishes. They struck a deal.

~~~~~~

Joe had hunted the morning at Jones Bluff, reporting to Connor that another gobbler had already taken the area in the other one's absence. "He's probably been there the whole season but was afraid to gobble much. He might have already been whipped by the other one a time or two," Joe said.

It comforted Joe to hear another gobbler there even though he'd failed to get a glimpse of him.

Over the next three days, the routine of living together became comfortable. Nancy enjoyed learning the new job. Connor had gained more friends at school since many of the students had seen him play ball. He continued to keep a comfortable, low profile there, preferring Janice's company over anyone else's.

Joe hunted every morning at different places except the Hall Place, where he'd started the season. Friday was the last day of the season and he planned to hunt there then.

Joe told Nancy about the appointment for tests at the hospital set for the following Tuesday. She insisted on asking Mrs. Baker for the morning off to drive to the hospital with her daddy. Joe had objected, but eventually gave in. Joe hated being a burden on other people.

On Thursday night, after Joe finished the dishes, he retired to the front porch with a final cup of coffee for the day.

Connor joined him on the porch.

"Paw Paw, I talked to a counselor at school today. She said she could help me with my plans for getting into Auburn. If I do what she says and make good grades until I graduate, she said she could almost guarantee I would be accepted. I'd like to go there. Maybe I can try out for their baseball team, too."

"That's good. If that's what you think you want to do. It's good to have a goal, but you need to stay focused on it."

Nancy joined them on the porch. "The whippoorwills aren't calling tonight."

"Not tonight, I think their season is about played out," Joe said.

"Well, I guess nothing lasts forever," she said.

The three of them sat on the porch enjoying the cool evening air. The breeze blew strong enough to keep the mosquitoes from biting too much. The stars shone through the tall trees across Rocky Hill Road.

Nancy silently pondered what, if anything, would last forever … love was the only thing she could think of.

CHAPTER 47 – SEASON'S CLOSE

Joe awoke Friday morning, setting his feet on the cool wooden floor before pushing the button to prevent the alarm clock from sounding. He padded to the kitchen to make coffee. Belle followed him into the kitchen as he stooped to fill her bowl with food. He petted her head as she wagged her tail.

Joe paused, rubbing his eyes. His energy had evaporated.

Turkey season has taken its toll on me.

He felt a little off balance. He missed his usual spark before hunting; his mind sputtering, like a badly tuned engine. But it was the last day of season. He had to go.

Joe parked the truck at the Hall Place and finished the cup of coffee. The moon rose above the trees. He lumbered to the special place before sitting against the longleaf pine. He closed his eyes, breathing in the warm air.

When the eastern sky lightened, a turkey gobbled from the hollow to his immediate front. Joe waited, listening for hens to call. They didn't. He cradled the cedar box call, sending two clucks. The tom answered right away.

Joe set the call on the ground, settling his back against the tree. He thought about the season, culminating on this day. Next season seemed far away. Joe already looked forward to it. This one had been so good. One of the best ones, in fact, when he considered it.

He thought about the changes the season had brought. Nancy would sell her house in Mobile soon, allowing her to buy a place near Uriah to raise the boy until he went to college. A good stand of corn grew in the field. Connor had turned a corner, now doing great in school. He had earned a position on the baseball team. Best of all, a turkey gobbled not a hundred yards in front of him.

The turkey gobbled five more times on his own from the roost before flapping wings signaled him flying to the ground. He saw the tom as it landed under a stand of dogwoods, fifty yards downhill. Joe's eyes blurred. He blinked to get them focused. His head tingled. His chest tightened.

The turkey began pacing straight toward him. Joe's pulse rushed the blood through his veins. His heart throbbed, struggling in his chest. His eyes blurred again. He strained to focus again as a pain between his shoulder blades increased. The tom continued toward him at twenty-five yards with its neck stretched high in the air.

Joe whispered aloud, "Shoot him, Connor … shoot him."

CHAPTER 48 – THE HUNT

When Connor arrived home from school, he didn't see Joe's truck. He opened the front door to yell, "Paw Paw?"

He waited a few minutes before deciding to call his mother at her work. "Paw Paw's not here. What should I do?" Connor said.

"That's not like him," Nancy said. "He didn't mention anything to me about going anywhere this afternoon. Did he say anything to you?"

Connor thought hard, "No, ma'am."

"Do you know where he went hunting this morning?" she asked.

"Yes, ma'am, back at the Hall Place. I'm gonna get somebody to take me there to see if his truck is still there."

"Okay, be careful. Write a note, in case he comes back. Let me know something as soon as you can."

Connor hung up. He wrote a note, leaving it on the kitchen table. The note read: Gone to Hall Place to look for you.

Connor rode his bike at full speed to the Johnson's house, explaining to Mr. Johnson why he needed a ride to the Hall Place. They rushed to the old truck, leaving along Rocky Hill Road.

~~~~~

In Monroeville, Nancy told Mrs. Baker about the situation, mentioning where Joe had gone hunting that morning.

Mrs. Baker called Jessie on the CB radio, learning Jessie worked only twelve miles away from the Hall Place. He told Mrs. Baker that he'd drive there to search for Joe's truck. She told Nancy to go home early. Nancy left work, rushing home.

~~~~~~~

After Mr. Johnson and Connor turned from the county road, they parked at the locked gate. Jessie Pickens pulled in directly behind them. Connor ran to the gate, climbing over in a rush. Mr. Johnson and Jessie followed behind.

After Connor ran another hundred yards along the road, he spotted Joe's truck before yelling back to the men. "Here's his truck. I know where he is." He ran through the woods toward Joe's special place.

Connor found Joe slumped to one side with his face locked tight against the stock of the old double barrel. Joe still held the gun with his left hand under the forearm, in the firing position. Connor didn't have to touch him; Paw Paw had been gone for a long time.

Connor emitted a low moan, as he turned in circles. The moan increased in volume with each revolution. Growing into an echoing scream, Connor began to wail. He knelt on his knees beside his grandfather's body, leaning back, crying openly up into the trees. Jessie came near, kneeling beside him, pulling the boy close to his big chest. Jessie held on tight … and wept.

Mr. Johnson stood behind them, choking back his own tears. His heart ached deeply for the boy. He dropped to his knees to say a silent prayer.

CHAPTER 49 – HOPE

The Baptist Church hosted a wake for Joe Parker on Sunday night. Crowds of people passed through the church before gathering in the yard. Connor, along with Nancy, sat still in the front row as the people filed by to express their condolences. Connor barely endured the evening.

The next day, before the funeral, the house filled with visitors, most bringing food to the house, an old Southern tradition. Several men set up tables under the shade trees in the front yard to support the overflow of food.

Janice sat with him for a while. They held hands right in front of everybody. They didn't talk much. There was no use in talking. That would come later. Janice understood.

The funeral service at the church passed as a blur in Connor's head. He remained reserved as his mother pulled him close. He knew the preacher would say good things about his grandfather but listened to little of the service.

Later that evening, when everyone drifted away from the house, Connor went outside on the front porch to sit beside his mother in the swing.

They sat in silence for a long time. A whippoorwill began to call. "Oh, they're back," Nancy said, wiping her eyes.

"Life ain't fair, Mama," Connor said.

"No, sir. Sometimes, it damn sure ain't." Nancy sniffed.

Connor had never heard his mother use the word *damn* before. He grasped his mother's hand, squeezing it. "Everything will be okay, Mama," he said as he considered her face. "Won't it?"

She gazed at Connor, "I promise. We're gonna make it, Connor. Through the sadness, through the changes. We'll make Daddy proud."

Connor imagined she meant her daddy *and* his daddy, at the same time. He laid his head on her shoulder as they listened to the last whippoorwill calls of nineteen sixty-nine.

Connor woke early the next morning. He made coffee like Joe liked it ... strong. He carried his cup to the front porch. Nancy slept late. Exhaustion had worn them down.

He finished the coffee before he strolled to the chicken pen to open the gate. As he approached the pen, the ole rooster crowed from his roost in the tall bushes.

Behind the field of corn, Connor heard a turkey gobble. He stopped to listen again to be sure it was real. Then, the turkey gobbled again.

Paw Paw said he had never heard a turkey around the house. There's never been any turkeys in this part of the woods. I know this for a fact.

Standing in the first light of morning, with the rooster crowing and the wild turkey answering from behind the cornfield, Connor was suddenly overwhelmed with ... *hope.*

It made no sense to him, yet it filled him ... deep inside.

That turkey is paying his respects to Paw Paw.

The thought made Connor recollect some things Joe had said:

Do it the right way... Do the right thing ... I'll still be with you.

Remembering his Paw Paw's words lifted his spirit. He smiled for the first time in several days.

Connor stood still for a long time, listening to the gobbler, its beautiful voice echoing through the surrounding woods.

EPILOGUE

Seven weeks later ... Tuesday morning

Connor came in through the backdoor. He put the eggs he'd gathered in the sink before scrubbing them.

It had been weeks since the funeral. Strangely, Paw Paw's death had not made Connor angry. He had lived a good life. But, Connor missed him with his whole heart.

Nancy wandered into the kitchen from the bedroom to stand beside him to help. "I'm accepting the offer on the Mobile house today."

"That's good." Connor smiled.

Nancy dried her hands with a dishtowel, putting her arm around Connor's shoulder, "You should take some of these eggs to the Johnsons."

"I'm planning on that tomorrow."

"Your Paw Paw would be proud."

"Yes, ma'am." Connor's chest expanded while gazing out the kitchen window.

"Chickens okay?"

"Yes, ma'am." He paused, gently biting his lip he turned to her, "When we remodel Paw Paw's house, can we get an air conditioner?"

Nancy chuckled, "We'll see. What time's the game Saturday?"

"Two o'clock. I have to be there at one."

Connor leaned over to feed Belle.

"I haven't heard that turkey behind the field again," he said.

"Well, gobbling season is over."

"Yes, ma'am. But there's always next year."

"Yep, there's always next year."

Nancy put the eggs in the refrigerator.

Connor and Nancy had settled in well to Uriah. Mrs. Baker's last week of work had just ended. Jessie had thrown a retirement party for her with over a hundred in attendance. Nancy loved her job and the hard-working, colorful saw-hands she had met.

Connor had a job after school two days a week unloading trucks and stocking shelves at the Big Store, insisting that he would buy two pigs soon with his own money. The corn crop was doing well and he was almost finished repairing the hog pen.

"The best way to learn sometimes is to make a plan and just go do it," Paw Paw had said. And, Connor McCoy had plans ... big plans.

ABOUT THE AUTHOR:

Alan White resides with his wife in his hometown in rural south Alabama. They have three children and three grandchildren.

The founder and editor-in-chief of Great Days Outdoors Magazine, which began publishing in early 1997. He is a member of the Southeastern Outdoor Press Association. Alan was named Conservation Communicator of the Year in 2014 in the Alabama Governor's Conservation Achievement Awards. Alan is an accomplished musician and songwriter.

He is the founder and chairman of Alabama Hunger Relief, a 501c3 charity which raises money to provide venison to food banks.

In his spare time, he enjoys time with his family, hunting, fishing, vegetable gardening, tanning animal skins, oil painting, and wildlife management.

One Season is Alan's first novel.